THE QUESTION OF SABOTAGE

OF

SABOTAGE

A FESTIVAL TALE

Bonnie J. Morris

THE QUESTION OF SABOTAGE

A FESTIVAL TALE

Bonnie J. Morris

Bella
BOOKS

Ferndale, Michigan
2001

Bella Books, Inc.
P.O. Box 201007
Ferndale, MI 48220

Printed in the United States of America on acid-free paper
First Edition

Editor: Lila Empson
Cover designer: Bonnie Liss (Phoenix Graphics)

This is a work of fiction, and all characters, incidents, and locations were invented by the author, with the exception of minor references to well-known celebrities or feminist organizations. There is no Amazon Womyn's Music Festival, nor is it intended to represent one specific festival from the many that have existed since 1974. Any resemblance to events or people at a festival you may have attended is purely coincidental.

Some material in chapter 1 was originally published in the author's *Eden Built by Eves*, Alyson Publications, 1999, and is reprinted with permission. Some material in chapter 4 was previously published as a short story, "The Festival Virgin," in two anthologies: *Hot Ticket*, edited by Linnea Due, Alyson, 1997, and *Electric*, edited by Nicole Foster, Alyson, 1999, and is also reprinted with permission.

ISBN 0-9677753-8-8

*Dedicated with great love to
my kind and funny, strong and loving friends
in festival culture, especially
my pals in the Campfest gazebo,
the Michigan worker community,
Darby Hoover, and
the lovely Laura B. Ripplinger*

Anticipation

I've never been to NEWMR or to Michigan
I won't drink beer from bottles/a glass I'll pour it in
I don't have any crystals/don't know my Yang from Yin
What kind of self-respecting lesbian am I?
      — Leah Zicari,
      from "Wouldn't That Be Fun?"

I never wear clothes and I feel comfy
At the women's festival in the country.
      — Zoe Lewis,
      from "I'll Be Ten Years Old,"
      August Night Café,
      Michigan Womyn's Music Festival.

1

Festival season begins in spring, but opening day is not honored by television newscasters. Hallmark does not acknowledge festival season on calendars or greeting cards. The federal government allows no paid holidays for festiegoers or performers; the White House sends no benevolent wishes for a happy festival season; retailers hang no placards urging shoppers to make their festival purchases *now*; drugstores, which feverishly change displays from Easter themes to Father's Day themes, do not pause to market festival season candies in honor of the nation's lesbian holidays.

Anticipation begins in secret.

See the large and well-stocked supermarket. Into its aisles go suburban homemakers and the occasional helpful dad. Affluent matrons inquire about meat. But wait! There, in aisle 12, three women are loading a shopping cart with flashlight batteries, biodegradable shampoo, toilet paper, insect spray, film, tampons, sex lubricant, lantern oil, sunscreen, and chocolate chip cookies. They have arguments: Is it more practical to pack powdered drink mix or to buy beverages once they arrive on the land? What's going on?

Across town, another woman is loading her camper with tents and sleeping bags, tarps and air mattresses, coolers and folding beach-chairs, while her lover, mending moth-eaten winter socks, yells from the front porch, "Don't forget the citronella candles and our fanny packs!"

In airports, ticket agents wrestle with amplifiers, electric guitars, computerized keyboards, Taiko drums, djembe drums, conga drums, while anxious performers scream, "No, no! Hold it up *that* way, please." A seven-member salsa band, temporarily stranded at O'Hare International Airport because of inclement weather, forms a circle and begins impromptu soccer juggling with a Hackey Sack ball right in the terminal.

Cars loaded with gear, with bumper stickers proclaiming I DID IT AT NEWMR and SEE YOU IN AUGUST, pull into gas stations for super unleaded and road munchies. "How many more miles to the turnoff?" wail plaintive, butch voices from

2

the backseat. Holly Near tapes blare from the auto stereo; a crystal swings from the rearview mirror. We know where this car is headed.

Running through each woman's mind, like documentary film loops, are her private hopes and fantasies, which have nurtured and savored festival images all winter long:

It's going to be awesome.

Maybe I'll meet someone this year.

Maybe that cool dreadlocks woman in the green sunglasses will be there again.

I'm going to stay up and party all night every night.

I'm going to attend all the performers' workshops until I finally get to shake Ferron's hand ... That's all I ask, Goddess ... I really want a radical haircut this time, and no kidding.

Gee, I wonder if the tattoo artist will take Visa?

I know I left my vibrator behind the kitchen pantry last year; somebody may have found it since then ...

How will I possibly be able to flirt with Pam now that Cougar's sharing our Winnebago?

I worked out all year to have buff biceps for this festival, and now she tells me to pack bulky sweaters for cold weather!

My very own set on the night stage ... Please, please, let me remain zit-free.

I can't wait. I can't wait. I can't wait ...

But in the mind of one festie-virgin, one Ceci Sobol, a different refrain cried out, taunting and defeated: *I'm going to hate it. I'm going to hate it in an extreme way. I don't know how to camp. I'm terrified of being left out by the in-crowd. I have too many allergies. So why did I let myself get talked into attending this fiasco?*

Chapter One

Circumstances strange creating new range of possibilities
Expectations deranged heart still caged wants new
compatabilities.
> — Amy Simpson,
> from "Circumstances Strange"

Friday morning on the land

Ceci glared at her reflection in the rearview mirror. Idling, dust-streaked cars lined the dirt road leading up to the festival gates. Women had driven from all over the United States and Canada to reach the Amazon Womyn's Music Festival on opening day, and the traffic jam stretched nearly back to the remote highway turnoff.

Bluefern, the festival's jaunty and competent head of security, was in her element walking up and down the road, wearing nothing but boxer shorts, an orange reflector vest, and an ankle brace. "Welcome! Welcome. Stay in line, please. Welcome to the Amazon Festival. All cars, stay to the right ahead; you'll be parked in Susan B. Anthony Field. Trucks and RV campers, go left at the gate and park in Harriet Tubman Pasture. Be sure you have your festival tickets ready. Hi, welcome, glad to see you again. You're almost there. Got your tickets? Got your rain gear? Hear we're due for one sprinkle Saturday night. Keep it moving. Welcome . . ."

On top of an unmoving RV at the back of the line, two women dozed in a large rubber life raft while a third, in the camper's small kitchen, made sandwiches.

Ceci and her new friend Melissa, who had offered her a ride to the festival from Boston, watched the odd parade from behind dirt-streaked Toyota windows. It was Ceci's first time at a women's music festival, and the small car groaned with her plaid baggage and physics textbooks. She wore stiff new red sneakers, blue jeans, and a white blouse. Melissa had removed all her clothing as soon as they'd made the highway turnoff.

"Oy, this will take forever," moaned Ceci, for whom breathing large quantities of road dust was less than an ideal situation.

"Once we're inside you'll love it. There'll be nearly three thousand women this year, and everyone walks around without a shirt!"

Ceci's aching head swam at the prospect of six thousand breasts. "I don't want to take off my clothes," she whispered.

"Relax, kiddo, you don't have to. You can do whatever you want. Now, we're going to set up my tent in Chemical-Free. That all right with you?"

5

Ceci, whose plaid overnight bag bulged with allergy medications and inhalers, wept, "But my Benadryl . . ."

"Oh no. No, look. Chem-free camping means no alcohol, no cigarette smoking, no recreational drugs. It doesn't mean your personal medicine. It's a camping area preferred by a lot of women in recovery, like me. No exposure to booze, and it's often quieter. Believe me, no one is going to take away your Benadryl."

Ceci watched as two athletic Japanese women with spiked hair and studded leather bracelets set up a sandpit volleyball court off to one side of the gate, then made love in it. "If my parents could see me now," she sighed.

"Yeah. Guess this is a different scene from the sterile old lab, huh?"

Ceci felt a stab of longing for the sterile old lab. A doctoral student at MIT, she had nervously entered New Words, the local women's bookstore in Cambridge, Massachusetts, to search for texts on women in science. There she'd been greeted with boisterous sisterhood by freckle-faced Melissa, who worked at the cash register. Melissa had described the upcoming women's music festival with touching reverence — and had spent nearly three-quarters of an hour urging Ceci to attend. She finally offered Ceci a ride across the country and space in her waterproof dome tent as well, since Ceci had no camping equipment of her own.

Ceci was grateful for Melissa's friendly, Boston-accented outreach, but fearful about the days ahead. Cold memories of being left out, made fun of, laughed at by bigger and stronger girls swirled like steam through Ceci's emerging lesbianism.

Would Melissa help her adjust to festival culture? Show her the ropes? Were ropes, in fact, involved in this apparently obligatory coming-out rite of festival attendance? Eyes glazing over from road dust, Ceci couldn't get the rope metaphor out of her imagination: S/M, survival courses, cowgirls busting broncs out West.

Oy, no ropes, please. Why was she here? Engulfed in a fresh cloud of exhaust, she reached for her bag of pills.

"Are you okay?" asked Melissa.

"Fine," Ceci sneezed in reply.

"My God, it's Bim! Did you see her?"

"Bim!"

"Bim's here!"

Adoring shrieks rose from the throng of cars as a sleek maroon minibus passed on the left and pulled up to the backstage gate. Bim Daring, the most popular performer scheduled to appear at the festival, climbed out of the bus and waved her trademark, custom-made left-handed guitar at her swooning admirers. "We love you, Bim!" called out a gray-haired fan from the back of a Harley-Davidson. A smaller shuttle van approached to take Bim and her equipment into the restricted Artists' Camping Zone.

Several yards away, rival performer Carrie Marathon was not pleased. "Bim! That bitch!" she seethed, clenching her banjo. "How does she get away with it? Ooh, I'd like to —"

"Take it easy," Carrie's road manager urged. "Here. Have a sip of soy milk."

"God damn it, I don't want soy milk. I knew Bim would be here, but why does she have to be the first performer I run into? I can't take much more."

"There, there," soothed Carrie's road manager.

"At least we don't perform on the same nights. Grr. That low-down, hypocritical . . . Do you know, she —"

"Hush," said the road manager, glancing at Bluefern.

* * * * *

Bluefern had not overheard any of Carrie's remarks and was, in fact, preoccupied with assisting traffic. As head of security, she could have given this job to one of her parking crew, but Bluefern loved opening day at the festival gates.

Up and down the rows of gritty cars, women were beaming, shouting greetings to old friends, breaking out wine coolers, pulling off city shirts to reveal brown and black shoulders. Yes, it looked good this year. No problems so far. Everyone happy to arrive, and clear weather holding.

Bluefern smiled as one carless woman, loaded with army-navy surplus gear and waterbags, strode methodically up the road in black boots. "I like your tattoos, sister!" called Bluefern.

The woman glanced fearfully behind her, then smiled briefly and trudged on.

"Local girl," Bluefern confided to the volleyball players. "Every summer we get these paranoid muscle dykes from the military base in the next county. They come here on their own free leave time and risk dishonorable discharge and worse. Usually there's a big purge at the end of summer at the base; they can pick out the ones who've come here by their allover tans. We tell them now to keep their shirts on, for their own anonymity later."

Having at last parked the Toyota, Melissa and Ceci were now at the registration and orientation tent, trying to choose from a wide spectrum of work-shift options. Until they signed up for a work shift, they wouldn't be able to get their meal tickets. The whole arrangement reminded Ceci of her mother's oft-told stories about the labor camps in Nazi Germany.

"Do you have any particular skills?" the work-shift coordinator asked Ceci.

8

"I have an honors degree in calculus, a master of science in particle theory, I'm a doctoral candidate in physics at MIT, and I can program sixteen computer systems," Ceci replied.

"Bev means skills that could be of use to us at this festival," called out a woman with strawberry-blond beard hairs.

"And, uh, I speak six languages," Ceci tried again.

"Oh. Fine. Well, you can do your work shift in the communications tent; we get a lot of international women here, both festiegoers and artists, needing translation. I don't suppose one of your languages is Japanese?" Bev asked, looking skeptically at Ceci's very Jewish face.

"*Hai!*" Ceci responded in near-perfect Japanese.

"Well, hot damn. All right, She-bear, radio down to Central that we've got a brainy one coming in."

"A brainy one," Ceci seethed and fumed, staggering after Melissa with her arms bent under a load of camping gear. "That woman called me a brainy one."

"If the shoe fits," chuckled Melissa, who had somehow ended up carrying all of Ceci's physics textbooks. "Who the hell does homework at a festival?" Twigs and pods and dead branches crackled under their feet as they plowed up the hill toward Chem-Free and Quiet Camping.

"It's research, not homework. I'm in graduate school, third year; we don't get weekends off. We read and study continually! You see? For better or for worse, I carry MIT's curriculum around with me until I have my doctorate in hand. I need to prepare for my oral exams. They're soon enough."

"Plenty of women on the land who'll coach you for oral examinations," Melissa teased.

* * * * *

9

Ceci looked terrified.

Never in her life on planet Earth had Melissa encountered such an unrepentant nerd. "Look, please. Cecilia. I didn't mean anything. And She-bear up at registration didn't mean anything. You shouldn't take our joking so hard. We're just busting your chops, just whaling on you, because you're an easy mark."

"Busting?" Ceci tried out the verb. "Whaling?"

"Hoo-boy." Melissa sat down on her rolled-up plastic ground cloth, suddenly aware that she was very far away from her old neighborhood where casual and elaborate insults were a way of life. "Okay, listen to me. This is just lesbian humor. Butch lesbian humor. You know anything about ghetto humor?"

"Of course," sniffed Ceci. "I told you that my parents were Holocaust refugees."

"Right. Fine, so you probably know that whether the group identity is rooted in race, ethnicity, or sexuality, an oppressed group develops a certain humor, a certain banter, as a way of facing down hardships?"

"I know all *that*."

"So dykes test and tease newcomers, like you. You know that in lots of inner-city communities black kids learn to play the dozens, the insult games, usually at the expense of somebody's mama, and you're obviously familiar with Yiddish humor, which specializes in _great_ insults at the expense of men."

"Like *shmuck*," Ceci agreed, slapping away mosquitoes.

"Well. Where I grew up we were surrounded by every last one of those wisecracks, from black, Jewish, Italian, and Polish cultures, and we learned a pretty tough neighborhood slang. But many lesbians also adapt this strategy of got-one-on-you talk as a way of flirting, of showing off, of imitating what once were breezy male attitudes. Working-class dykes are also a kind of ghetto subculture, you'll see. We try to sound tough, as well as tender."

10

"So to greet a new woman you might like, you're supposed to insult her?" Ceci demanded. *"Bust* on her? Create semantic booby-traps, to which she must respond? That's not my nature. It's more your way, your manner."

"Sometimes it's just the teasing ways that butches talk to butches," Melissa suggested with a smile. "Or try to get a rise out of shy babes, like you."

"I'm not really what anyone would call butch."

"No shit, Sherlock."

They trudged along in silence, then entered a glen ringed with dry tree stumps. "This is perfect!" announced Melissa, and Ceci immediately sat down and blew her nose.

Within a few brisk minutes, Melissa had set up her sturdy dome tent complete with rain tarp and air mattresses, while Ceci studied a field guide to poisonous plants and insects and sneezed. "You can come in here and lie down now, if you like," Melissa called through the tent's screened window. Leaf shadows made geometric shapes on the nylon walls, making their temporary shelter looked restful.

Together, they read through the festival program, which listed concert schedules and workshops for the weekend. "This sounds fucking awesome," Melissa enthused, circling *Clean and Sober Athletes* and *City Jazz Jam* with a red marking pen. "We have plenty of time to wander around, maybe take in a few workshops, before dinner and the night stage. What looks good to you?"

"I, ha, yes, well, " sputtered Ceci, trying to appear cool and experienced while inwardly reeling from the erotically explicit titles of some workshops: *Proudly Polyamorous, Intro to Flogging, Sex Toys for the New Millennium.* "Perhaps I won't go to any one workshop today, but just wander around, observe. Um, take notes." Ceci glanced at the naked Melissa and blushed. She whipped out her nose drops. "Seriously, Melissa, what on earth are these workshops supposed to prove or accomplish? Listen to this: *'Breast Art.* Using our own breasts and nontoxic paints, we will make designs and greeting cards for the festival gallery.' Or this one: *'Unlearning Suzuki.* For radical feminist musicians who need to break free from formal methodologies and training.' I mean! Surely with so many women gathered in one place we might strive for quality discussions and exchanges of ideas. I had hoped to meet other women in science here."

"Start your own workshop then," Melissa invited. "You can do whatever you please here, really. Why not put up a sign for *Asthmatic Science Nerds and the Women Who Love Them*? Then you can have your quark and get eaten too."

"Shut up," Ceci protested.

"Oh, get over it, girlchild. Come on, let's explore. Most of the activities and festival services are down in the central field; I'll show you."

Ceci hiked alone through thick foliage, much of which was already crowded with tents. Ceci saw women setting up elaborate supper grills at private campsites, hanging up portable solar showers, affixing clotheslines between tree branches.

Two women appeared to have brought a small Persian rug and woven mats to grace their tent entryway. "I must be outta my mind, Abby, to let you bring a rug into the woods," Ceci overheard one member of this couple scold.

"Yeah, yeah," her partner replied, "But you know. I *have* to create a familiar environment for myself, first thing, or I'll never be able to focus. Rugs keep me sane; a blow dryer would be even better. Is it my fault I grew up in New Jersey?"

Ceci felt better.

Eventually the path turned toward a clearing and Ceci could see booths, some cabin structures, larger tents, and a performance stage. Many women had arrived on the land the previous evening and were already at ease, strolling through the Crafts area, munching on snow cones, comparing workshop options in their festival programs. It might have been any outdoor crafts fair and folk concert *milieu* in rural America, except that naked breasts predominated. In glorious variety, Ceci thought.

"Gevalt!" Ceci heard herself marvel.

She saw white-haired women with creased faces and strong hands; toddling girl children beaming through smeared finger paint; women of fine bulk and women of thin sinew; deaf women and interpreters signing their conversations in urgent grace.

Black, brown, tan, golden, red, pink, and white skins glistened in folds and ripples, their sheen spiraling outward from the central configuration of breasts and bellies.

Enormous breasts like full and intricate baggage; smaller breasts erect and goose-bumped by wind; breasts marked or altered by cancer surgeries; breasts stretched from lactation and some, presently, swollen with milk for the nourishment of a dangling girl-child.

Muscles and veins ran strongwise beneath the rolling flesh. Sunburned white women ruefully atoned for yesterday's nudity, women rubbing lotion onto one another's chests with glad palms.

Never in her life had Ceci seen more than one naked body, maybe two, at a time; and this was *nothing* like the redwood sauna at the gym. Automatically, Ceci glanced down at her still-covered breasts, wondering if she could feel the confidence necessary to cast aside her shirt and join the mammary-gland revue.

As she walked carefully among the topless festiegoers, the smell of a thousand body oils, anointments, and perfumes filled Ceci's nostrils, irritating her sensitive membranes, yet conveying a subtler message of adult female sensuality that was pleasing to heart and mind.

Well trained in chemical analysis from her years of laboratory experiments, Ceci quickly recognized the individual scents dabbed on different women's bare necks . . . scents she had associated, in the past, with various lovely and unattainable women assigned to her as lab partners.

Ah, there was musk oil, patchouli, eucalyptus, Eternity, Jontue, Cachet, orange-blossom, White Shoulders, rosewater, Millionaire, Love's Baby Soft, Chanel, Youth Dew, and Arpege — and, radiating upward from the sun-warmed breasts of women lying down, a secondary wave of Hawaiian Tropic, Coppertone, Nivea, baby powder, aloe, lanolin, and Noxzema.

Barely had Ceci's brain (and nostalgia for coveted girls) quantified all of this information when her sense of smell went out of commission for the rest of the day with one final sneeze.

As Ceci walked slowly into the village of bright skins, she overheard many incomprehensible conversations:

"Amy wants to know if the tempura's okay for vegans."

"Have the trash queens been through here yet? No? Whose crew is that? Well, tell her that the heat dried out all the tape and that the Naiad Press flyers fell off the Porta-Janes and are blowing around through the Womb."

"We need batteries for two chairs up at Differently Abled."

"Darn it! I forgot to bring the loofahs. And don't you dare suggest that we use my brand-new menstrual sponge in the shower."

"Hey, killer do. When did you get a bi-level?"

". . . then she left ACOA for NA, and then apparently blew off her program entirely, because I saw her with doobie in hand at P'town last month. A shame."

"I want a tofu dog and a Rice Dream, and after that we can do the Wicca workshop if you're done shopping for labryses and stuff."

"Have you seen any videos by the Lavender Fillies? Hot!"

"Go over to Rumor Control and ask if it's true that the 'terps have their own tent this year. These CODAs want to know."

Jargon. Acronyms. Initialisms. Insider language, thought Ceci, instantly resenting the terminology she could not yet understand. Here was a social dialect evolved from lesbian culture, from a dozen lesbian cultures, a dialect of struggle and womanly agency that accommodated female diversity.

T-shirts, bumper stickers, pins, and coffee mugs advertised different political causes, each spelling *woman* or *women* differently.

Impassioned commitment seemed to be tidily reduced to short notation: NOW, DOB, ASL, CODA, S-M, ACT UP, NARAL, GLAAD.*

Equations, abbreviations, and translations were old hat in Ceci's lab at MIT, where an enormous poster featuring the periodic table of chemical elements dominated the room. Perhaps the slogans and initialisms were not unlike mathematical and scientific formulas.

But the social language of lesbian culture was, for inexperienced Ceci, as frustrating and mysterious as atomic formulas might be to a nonscientist. Ceci had developed her present command of symbolic mathematics and nuclear physics through reading texts. Hundreds of books, journals, papers, articles; how many at last count? She had given up keeping a three-by-five file card on every completed study assignment. It was complicated enough to file away the knowledge in her own brain. Even computer science, which involved programming delicate machinery, could be learned from textbooks and then practiced.

But the language of festival culture? That was alive, animate, demanding participation and experience. She'd had no dictionary of festival slang to study before walking into this

*National Organization for Women; Daughters of Bilitis; American Sign Language, Children of Deaf Adults; sadomasochism; AIDS coalition to Unleash Power; National Abortion and Reproductive Rights Action League; Gay and Lesbian Alliance Against Defamation

world of tofu and 'terps. Ceci's proficiency in German, Yiddish, Hebrew, Russian, French, Japanese, IBM, and Macintosh could not bail her out of festival illiteracy.

Lesbian communication probably could not be boiled down to a professional, academic learning method, Ceci recognized; one had to live as a lesbian to understand the contours, the apt purpose, of lesbian slang.

Damn it all to hell, Ceci thought bitterly. Must I always be an outsider? The daughter of Holocaust survivors, she had grown up well aware of her family's place in Christian society, participating in sober adult discussions about insider-outsider culture from an early age. Nazi Germany had represented perhaps the ultimate "insiders' club," a club so specific and lethally empowered that nonmembers were killed en masse.

Yet Ceci's own refusal to date or marry a nice Jewish boy made her an outsider in conservative Jewish culture as well; *lesbische, lesbit, schanda fur leiten*, a scandal for the neighbors.

It mattered not to the shocked friends of Ceci's parents that lesbians, too, perished in Nazi death camps, forced to wear black triangles that marked women as "antisocial," meaning they had refused to marry and reproduce for the Fatherland.

Ceci's parents, with their crushing experiences as outsiders in Germany, also were outsiders in the United States — as Jews, as immigrants, as German-accented refugees. They watched in horror, wringing their still-tattooed hands, as anti-Semitic campaigns flared through both white and black American politics in the 1980s and 1990s.

When Ceci announced to her parents that she intended not to marry, they were thunderstruck: Why invite further trouble? Hadn't the family seen enough persecution? Ceci, raised American, with her good grades and her American accent could succeed here, even as a Jew. But to be lesbische? An outcast, an outsider, always.

Ceci had moved tentatively toward the idea of joining a

Jewish lesbian support group. There were several in Boston. Still barely out, she felt too shy to call the support group phone numbers listed in *Sojourner*. She had never had a real girlfriend, just crushes, fantasies, glimpses of possibility, like sweet dreams in the long night of university training.

It had not quite occurred to Ceci that one could "practice" a lesbian identity without having a lover. And thus she had missed out on the rallies, the women's music concerts, the recreational events that weren't quite sex time and weren't quite academic time. In graduate school, Ceci had pared away most of that middle ground called living, scheduling herself into either lab work or sleep.

Now, struggling to translate the peculiar conversations all around her in the bright field, Ceci realized that lesbian culture was simply a genre with resident experts controlling dialects and fads. She felt simultaneous irritation and amusement, knowing it would not take her long to pick up the language. It seemed that every subculture in America had its rules. Even presumably fun-oriented subcultures like surfing relied on surfer language, dress, and mannerisms off the beach. Likewise, apparently, lesbians used specifically lesbian airs and words out of bed.

Fine. But Ceci feared the elitism that often accompanied such insider talk. She feared being given, if she had to ask for the meaning of a word, the smug reply all brainy girls loathe: "You mean you don't *know*?"

But how could she possibly participate in this festival and win much-needed social experience if she didn't understand any of the directions, titles, conversations?

Why did everyone seem to be speaking Festivalese, louder and louder?

"Yeah, we broke up. Liz thought I was too vanilla."

"Oh, the Olivia Cruise was great! If only we hadn't run out of dental dams . . . You know, it's true that there's always *too much to eat* on a cruise . . ."

"Crystal healing at three. Then a dramatic reading of the

17

SCUM Manifesto at the Seps Tent. Then my coven is playing softball over by the Loud and Rowdy Zone. After that I could meet up with you for dinner, but I promised to watch night stage with my ex-lover. You know it's her last time here — she's becoming a man."

I need to get out of here, thought Ceci, the spectacular collage of women's breasts and faces seeming to whirl around her head like a planetary orbit. I also need to wee. Dizzily, she moved toward the nearest of the well-trafficked Porta-Janes.

When Melissa returned to their dome tent later, she found Ceci weeping into her plaid sleeping bag.

"What's wrong?" Melissa moved quickly to massage Ceci's back. "Was it something I said?"

Breathing with some difficulty, Ceci swung into a cross-legged position and looked at Melissa through reddened eyes. "It was the turds," she explained in a faint voice. "They were just piled up ... too high." She swallowed. "I want to go home ... I need my own room, and my hypoallergenic blanket!"

"Oh, honey, don't let a Porta-Jane bring you down," came the annoyingly cheerful reply. "Look, I fell into a temporary toilet structure at one festival, and I keep coming back. The main rule is, when you're using a Porta-Jane, never look down."

"I feel so dirty," wailed Ceci.

"It's understandable. But you know you can take a nice shower here, before dinner, if you like. That's probably the best thing for you, cool you down, get that dust out of your nose, and then we'll meet for dinner before the show begins. All right?"

Ceci heaved a sigh and wiped at her eyes with a tissue.

"All right, already. I'm ruining your good time with all my whining. It's my mishegoss, my problem. It's just that . . . naked women are out there playing hug-tag in the poison oak! Doesn't anyone stop to think about safety any more?"

Chapter Two

Here we sit together, alone in our respective silences.
— Lynn Thomas
from "Courage"

Our survival depends upon our *not* being predictable.
— Alix Dobkin,
at Crone's Harvest Bookstore

Friday evening on the land

Ceci, having recovered from her initial horror at the
Porta-Jane situation, stood resignedly in a long line of naked
women, waiting to shower at five P.M.

She felt rather silly in her old plaid bathrobe and rubber-toed sneakers, but preferred not to remove all her clothing until the last possible moment. It was frightening enough to shower in front of hundreds of attractive women, none of whom she knew.

Everyone else in the long shower line seemed relaxed and comfortable, slapping their lovers' behinds with colorful towels, comparing tattoos, carefully removing sterling silver labrys jewelry, piercings, and wristwatches. The ferns surrounding the outdoor shower stalls were pale with dried toothpaste spit and shampoo suds.

Sitting atop blue milk crates, two women of African descent skillfully wove tiny seashells into one another's braids.

And then Ceci heard, floating, like clear bubbles of sound from somewhere hidden in the woods, women's voices raised in prayer. A group of Jewish women were welcoming in the Sabbath. The songs and blessings were immediately familiar to Ceci, and she felt a rush of relief and affection. At the same moment, a large woman in front of Ceci turned around, a beaded Star of David swinging between brown breasts; she, too, looked in the direction of the prayer service. Then she studied the row of industrial showerheads. Ceci followed her gaze with growing comprehension and shock. The woman caught Ceci's eye, and slowly muttered "Holy shit."

Everything came together in the crystallized salt of recognition for Ceci. No wonder she felt uncomfortable at the festival. After a lifetime of listening to her parents' vivid descriptions of their time in concentration camp, Ceci was automatically programmed to see images of the Holocaust in even the safest, most benign and welcoming of environments.

Technically, her scientific brain understood that this festival *required* security guards at every post to protect the assembled lesbians; *required* cheap accessible outdoor showers so that women of varying abilities could quickly wash and go; *required* temporary toilet structures so that the land could

21

accommodate thousands of women's waste over a short weekend.

But Ceci's emotional cues rang out bells of alarm at the sight of long lines of naked women moving patiently toward bare showerheads. In another place, another time, Ceci's own mother had stood naked in such a line, snatched away from death at the very last minute when Allied forces arrived. Ceci's own mother had spent her adolescence cleaning the concentration camp equivalent of Porta-Janes, under the watchful eye of women security guards who were considerably less benevolent than Bluefern's crew.

And Ceci's own mother had later hidden in very different woods, singing the Sabbath blessings despite the risk of such ritual, despite the loss of faith her peers had experienced.

Ceci's knees began to shake.

"Come on," the woman in front of Ceci declared, dropping an armload of towels, loofahs, and underwear and steering Ceci out of the shower line. Ceci followed numbly as the strong brown woman strode into the woods toward the direction of the Sabbath songs. In a small clearing, where a jagged stump served as a natural altar, ten women were lighting white candles.

"Got any extras?" Ceci's shower-line companion asked quietly. She took the two candles offered her, set them carefully upon the protective tinfoil covering the tree stump, and held a lighted match to the wax-encrusted wicks. "Brucha at ela," she invoked, and the other women in the clearing smiled.

Ceci recognized the blessing, but the Hebrew was different. It's feminized, she realized. She's blessing God as one woman addressing another woman. She's bringing in the Sabbath as commanded by the Goddess!

Fascinated, Ceci watched as her new friend, still stark-naked except for burgundy flip-flops, moved her hands ritually around the candle flames and then covered her eyes. How many times have I seen my mother do that? thought Ceci.

What would it be like if my mother prayed naked, outdoors, calling upon a woman god? What would it be like for me to do so?

Automatically she chanted "Amen" as the other woman finished the *mitzvah* of lighting the candles that distinguishes the Sabbath from the workweek, one of three commandments in Jewish law specifically entrusted to Jewish women.

Two other women in the gathering produced ceramic cups engraved with many symbols, one cup filled with wine, one cup filled with kosher grape juice.

The youngest woman present made the blessing over the cups. Another woman magically pulled a full loaf of challah from her knapsack and blessed the bread. Everyone took a sip from their "wine" of choice and then laid hands on the bread, ripping it ecstatically into bite-size chunks.

"Ailailailailailailail," a wild-haired older woman suddenly ululated on an earsplitting note.

Ceci found herself being folded into the arms of her shower-line sister, who shouted "Shabbat shalom, kiddo!" Then, suddenly, all twelve of them were dancing, linking hands, and doing a modified hora around the glowing stump. Twigs cracked and snapped beneath their pounding Birkenstocks.

Half an hour later, Ceci and her new friend Trudy, now covered in sweat and leaves and breadcrumbs, were back in the shower line. "I don't know about you, doll, but I really needed that," declared Trudy, picking her discarded shampoo and soap articles out of the ferns. "I was going to light candles at dinner, later, but this was a much better party."

"How did you learn the feminine version of the prayer service?" asked Ceci. They were nearly at the shower faucets now.

"Well, let's see. I lived with an Israeli dyke for a while, but anyone who's been through Hebrew school can play with male and female pronouns. Actually, the whole Sabbath scene is highly feminine, traditionally. You welcome the Sabbath

Queen; you invoke images of the divine presence, the Shekhinah, who is a female representation of God; and women and girls are commanded to light candles. But what a trip to have a Friday night service in women-only space!" Trudy sprang into the next available shower and pulled on the faucets. "Wowee, that's cold!" she gasped.

Ceci shyly disrobed and, quivering, forced herself under an adjacent showerhead. "Oy. Eee," she squealed.

"Nipple-stiffening, ain't it?" grinned a security worker who, still in her orange vest, was lathering her equally orange pubic hair. It was hard to imagine anyone as a Nazi now. After the initial shock, the strong cool water actually felt lovely on Ceci's tired sunburned body. She shut her eyes and let the spray flatten her hair against her face. "This is the only time my hair is ever straight," she remarked for perhaps the thousandth time in an ethnically lived life.

"Yeah? My hair's the only straight thing about me," said a proud Latina lesbian on the other side of Ceci.

All around them were the sounds of women singing, of women brushing one another's hair, of sexual banter and compliments. I can do this, thought Ceci; I'm a part of this. I'm a lesbian too. A Jewish lesbian who dances in the woods. She opened her eyes to thank Trudy for recognizing her sense of dislocation, for bringing her into what felt like safe and loving Jewish turf. But Trudy was gone.

Dinner was served from five to seven, and most women had already eaten by the time Ceci and Melissa entered the food line. Melissa hurriedly piled tofu, corn, and watermelon on her tin plate and began edging toward the outdoor stage area.

"Where are you going?" wailed Ceci, beginning to feel a fresh wave of panic as she surveyed the unfamiliar menu. Tempe? Soy cheese? Safflower butter? Rice cakes with yeast?

At home with her parents, *Shabbes* dinner included chicken and potato kugel and fish; at MIT, she usually ate out on Fridays. Ceci moved down the dinner line until she found soup and lentil stew and then stumbled after Melissa, who appeared hellbent on finding a good seat for the night concerts.

"Slow down!" Ceci barked at the back of Melissa's head as the two of them picked their way through a blankets and lawn chairs. To Ceci's dismay, a portion of her dinner-plate lentils spilled off, falling into the cleavage of a slumbering woman underfoot.

At last Melissa seemed satisfied that they could move no closer to the stage and still remain in chem-free seating. She unfurled a thick green quilt and plopped down, arranging her dinner, pillow, tiny insulated cooler of orange sodas, and binoculars. Ceci collapsed onto the quilt with an exhausted wheeze, just as the emcee for the evening walked out on stage and bellowed, "Welcome back to the Amazon Womyn's Music Festival!"

"Wheee-aaa," everyone howled back enthusiastically.

"I'm your emcee, Laverne, and first we have a few announcements," the woman on stage continued. "Please respect the seating in front of the stage, which is reserved for women who are deaf and for women in wheelchairs. If you wish to dance to the music, do so over by the snack bar.

"Please be sure to pick up your garbage after tonight's set; there are specially marked recycling bins for soda cans throughout the land. Workshop changes will be posted at the information tent by nine A.M. tomorrow.

"Oh, and everyone, please listen to this one. We have a Honda Civic with its lights on up in the parking lot, Ohio plates, bumper sticker saying MY OTHER CAR IS A BROOM." At least forty women rose and headed out, certain this was their car.

Laverne shuffled through some papers at the mike stand. "There's been a request for a chiropractor at health care. Now.

We need fifty more women for overnight security, and I'm sure you'll all sign up with Bluefern as soon as you've finished your dinners. Hey, check it out, gals, security's fun. You get to wear an orange vest and eat free granola bars; it's a happening kind of scene. And we need your woman-energy to keep this festival safe!

"Tonight we have a special treat. First we'll be hearing from that great country-and-western band, the Bolo Ties, and then after a short intermission we'll welcome back Bim Daring!"

"Yea-a-a," shrieked the crowd.

"Bim's been a favorite at this and other festivals for many years now, and we were lucky to get her for our opening-night set. She's got a new album out, and tomorrow you can buy it — and meet Bim — when she does a signing at Ladyslipper!"

"What on earth does that mean?" inquired Ceci, through a mouthful of stew. "A signing at Ladyslipper?"

"Ladyslipper is a women's music distribution company. The other one is Goldenrod. They both have a booth here with records and CDs and tapes for sale, and most performers stop by to autograph tapes the day after a concert." Melissa chuckled. "I guess there are a lot of in-group expressions that sound alienating to a festie-virgin."

And that's another one of them, Ceci thought to herself, weary of being addressed as festie-virgin and baby dyke. Aloud she said, "Well, so far I've learned *Porta-Jane*, *Chem-Free*, and, ah, the *Womb*."

"*Shuttle*," added Melissa.

"*Trash queens*," chimed in a woman sitting behind them. "And *differently abled*."

"That's a term you hear outside of festivals," corrected a woman with crutches, to Ceci's left. "And a lot of us don't even like it."

"*TAB*," grinned the lover of the woman with crutches. "That means 'temporarily able-bodied.' "

"*Heterosexist. Heteropatriarchy. Terps*, for 'interpreters.' "

26

"*Crone. Croning ceremony*— you know, when it's some dyke's fiftieth birthday."

"*LST*. 'Lesbian standard time,' " called out somebody else, and so it went throughout the group of women seated nearest Ceci and Melissa, everyone contributing festival words, cultural code words, political terms popular with festival audiences and producers.

Ceci, eager to create her own lexicon of Festivalese, hastily jotted down the expressions as she heard them, and added to her notebook what she remembered of Trudy's gender-bendered Hebrew. She raised her pen with a wicked smile. "I've got one. *Gender-bender!*"

The sun had set completely by the time of the Bolo Ties' fourth number, and a few flashlights appeared as latecomers beamed their way into the concert field. Melissa, at her ninth festival and completely comfortable, chugged orange soda and tapped her feet. Ceci began to feel damp and cramped, and added one layer of clothing after another until she resembled a well-padded billikin. Melissa looked at her and roared. "You'll never be able to dance in all that!"

"Who says I'm going to get up and dance at all?" Ceci retorted. She suddenly remembered being in the woods that afternoon, doing the hora, Trudy's hand in hers. Tiny lumps of arousal formed just below her armor. "Maybe I've *already* danced," she informed Melissa, not a little smug.

The Bolo Ties finished their set with an accompanying display of country-and-western dancing, performed by two proficient women dressed in high cowgirl elegance. While the set crew moved microphone stands and drums, Laverne returned to the stage to announce raffle winners.

Ceci listened with interest for her own name, then realized she had forgotten to buy a raffle ticket. Still, it was rather fun to hear, in the names of winners, the ethnic and geographic variety of women at the festival: Eve Blackdaughter from Delaware ... Lora Jimenez from Florida ... Moon Stokowski from New York ... Genevieve Broussard from Quebec.

And the prizes! Gold and silver jewelry, hand-carved music rattles, silk scarves, wind chimes, Tarot readings. The announcement of each raffle winner was followed by delighted howls from the lucky woman and her friends in far corners of the lawn, little explosions of triumph that set others laughing in empathy.

There was a good-natured feeling to the opening night show, an infectious camaraderie even Ceci could not resist. She found herself lying back in the soft weeds, watching stars and constellations appear in the sky above.

How much more moving and powerful those stellar formations looked here, over the upturned faces of robust women, than in the advanced astronomy classes where Ceci had studied the stars! She quickly found Orion's Belt, Cassiopeia's Chair, the Pleiades, the Big and Little Dippers, Venus, Mars, the Milky Way, and the first brilliant streaks of Perseid meteor showers.

Suddenly there a shooting star flashed so bold and delicate that nearly all the women seated in the outdoor field glimpsed its tail and cried out in loud admiration. Laverne, on stage, in the midst of telling a poor joke involving kd lang and Martina Navratilova, looked out in astonishment at the cheering women and said, "Gee, I didn't think the punch line was that good."

Backstage, Bim Daring was not a happy folksinger. With one sleek hand on her custom-made guitar, she paced up and down in annoyance, looking for her Artist Care worker. "Damn it, Bluefern, where in hell is Rachel? She's supposed to be here to watch my stuff while I'm on stage. She's supposed to bring me my snack afterward. She's supposed to carry my extra guitar picks!"

Bluefern was also annoyed by Rachel's disappearance, but her immediate priority was to pacify Bim and get the show started. "Here," she suggested, "We'll have one of the stage crew set out your guitar, set out the picks, set out some water. Then you can make your entrance as soon as you hear the tape begin." Bim's first song of the evening would be performed to a backup tape from her last album. "After your set, I'll be sure to have a snack ready. That everything you need?"

"I guess so," Bim sighed. "Sorry, Bluefern. You know how I get, needing everything to be completely under control." Her eyes narrowed. "You know that Carrie Marathon is here; she'd just love to see me trip up on stage."

"Ah. I remember the good old days when you two opened this festival together," Bluefern risked pointing out. "We all loved those concerts. Do you think you'll ever work out whatever went wrong between the two of you, and tour together again? Not that it's any of my business, but —"

"No way," said Bim, closing the subject. She pushed gel through her hair and snapped impatiently at her suspenders while the stage workers finished preparations. Then, at a cue from the sound crew, Bim took the steps up to the stage as the first notes to her last hit recording filtered out from the monitors.

Something's wrong, Bluefern realized. Wait a minute. That cable looks loose. Hey. There's a cable sliding down from the — In that instant, with a brain-grating roar of feedback, the sound and light power crashed simultaneously, all the microphones went dead and, as the stage fell dark in hideous confusion, two hands quietly reached out and helped themselves to Bim's guitar.

* * * * *

Out in the field, the festiegoers screamed with dismay. Ceci and Melissa were unsure what had happened. Above them in the sound and light booth, workers were frantically throwing switches and turning knobs, to no avail. "Jesus H. Christ!" gasped one sound mixer to another. "Someone's cut the power."

"Someone's cut the power," Ceci repeated to Melissa.

"Some *man*'s cut the power?" another woman misunderstood.

"Some *man*'s cut the power!"

It became a shuddering chant.

A level-headed young couple immediately pulled on thick hiking boots and ran to the front of the field, urging everyone to shine her flashlight at the stage, to replace the lost lights.

Workers in the sound booth climbed down a few rungs, waving their own power flashlights before them. "No, Donna, no!" called the lighting designer from up top. "Don't go any farther. There's a live wire down there!"

With shrill exclamations, women in the audience backed away from the stage and the sound booth, now shining flashlights chaotically in every direction to check for severed cables and live wires. Then the stampede began, a few concerned festiegoers and workers surging forward, trying to get backstage to find out what had happened, and the great majority packing up in paranoid mob contagion, fearing the worst, lacking information and instructions.

Dust boiled up in clouds as everyone fled through the flashlight-slashed dark. Security workers struggled to assist women in wheelchairs who were at risk of being knocked over or of tripping others.

Terrified and unable to breathe, Ceci pulled her wool hat completely over her head and rolled into a ball on Melissa's blanket as legs and feet pushed past them. "No, no! Don't step on me!" she cried out as several women almost trampled her in passing. "Melissa! Help me!"

"Would everybody just calm down?" Melissa shouted in her best lifeguard-authority voice, but nobody heard.

At the side of the stage, Bluefern had leaped up just in time to see two sparking cables dangling from the canvas roof before everything went dark. Throwing down her walkie-talkie, she pushed up the stairs and found a battery-powered spotlight to focus on the stage. Bim stood aghast in confusion, two enormous sweat circles forming under her arms.

"Get away from the microphone stand!" Bluefern yelled before taking Bim's arm and steering her off the stage.

"It's not the whole festival," another security worker called over her shoulder as she carried a card table full of open water coolers away from the stage. "Look over at the Political Tent and at Childcare. They have power."

"Here you go," scowled Josie, Bluefern's petite second-in-command, probing at the foot of the stage. "Someone cut the main sound wire and slashed up the light cables. Oh, and groove on this, girls: Looks like Bim's microphone was hooked into one of the tampered wires. If she'd turned on her guitar juice and then grabbed the mike stand, she'd be teriyaki now."

"Christ," sobbed Bim, turning with an involuntary whimper to throw up on Laverne.

The festival producers, Nicky and Roslyn, careened up to the backstage area in their lavender golf cart. "What the hell happened, Bluefern?" yelled Roz from the driver's seat.

"Sabotage," said Bluefern. "Looks like we have an enemy on the land."

Two hours later, while a skilled crew of workers respliced cables and restored technical power at the night stage, Josie borrowed the producers' golf cart and buzzed smartly about the land, shouting through a bullhorn. "Everything's under control! The power has been fixed! There is no evidence of a man on the land! The security crew is keeping round-the-clock watch! Tomorrow's concerts will go on as scheduled! Thank you for your cooperation! Everything is under control!"

At midnight, close by the night stage, campfires blazed urgently in the workers' camp as Roz, Nicky, and Bluefern addressed an emergency meeting of the festival crew.

"Everything is not under control," began Bluefern. "Our electricians have determined that several sound and light cables were deliberately cut. Fortunately, we not only have backup cable, but we also have backup generators since we're renting a summer camp facility. If we were on private, woman -owned land without permanent structures, we'd be far less able to bounce back.

"The safety of our festiegoers is the key concern here. My crew can keep watch full-time for the rest of the weekend, but regardless of how well we protect the stages and the technical equipment, our saboteur may strike again at another source. And I do think it's a female saboteur; no man would have been able to get that close at the last minute without being spotted, so whoever was screaming that a man had cut the power was wrong.

"I don't like to alarm y'all, but suppose this loose cannon among us tries tampering with the food next? Or with all our cars up in the parking lots?"

"Bluefern, as head of security, do you have a large enough crew to post at all these sensitive areas?" asked Roz.

"I do, actually. Dozens of women have offered support and time, in addition to those who already signed up for security work shifts. Therein lies the problem."

"Oh my God, I see your point," sighed a young cook. "We rely almost entirely on volunteer labor, training anyone who signs up for a security shift. How do we know the saboteur isn't among the volunteers? With that in mind, there's no way we can assure security!"

"Right," affirmed Bluefern. "In fact, because the cables were cut right under our noses tonight, I have to assume that our troublemaker was on a stage work crew today. Or land crew. She could even be a member of our inner circle of staff here. She could be present at this moment."

Expletives, dismay, and anger circulated throughout the group.

"Look," Nicky interrupted, "There are several issues we must address. One is how to reestablish trust: among ourselves, and between the festival workers and the festiegoers. The last thing we need is a prolonged series of confrontations where we all look at one another with paranoid eyes and demand 'Are you the one?' or 'Where were you yesterday at four P.M.?' That would be really destructive to the sense of community we've built up over time. And I for one intend to keep on producing this festival and employing the women I've relied on for years.

"If we raise the question of whether there are agents among us, well, then we risk the fragmentation experienced at some of the peace camps, for instance, where women suspect their own lovers of being FBI infiltrators."

"Yeah, but how else will we find the woman responsible?" another worker yelled from the back row of the campfire circle.

"Assuming it's a woman," she added.

"*Could* it have been some disguised guy? What about the men who clean out the Porta-Janes? What about someone from town who decided to wreck our festival?" several voices called at once.

Bluefern rattled a shekere for attention. "There are no men on the land that I know of. I'm not going to make every woman strip off and show me her labia, either. The sanitation servicemen who clean out the portable bathrooms haven't

33

been here yet, as anyone can tell from the present state of our Porta-Janes. Face it, gals. Some messed-up festival babe fucked us over."

"What about Bim's guitar?" asked the cook. "It was stolen tonight during all the confusion. A separate crime? Or part of the weird-ass plot? We might have a cable-slicing thief, or a cable-slicer and an accomplice thief, or a thief who just needed to make a distraction in order to get a left-handed guitar."

"I've spoken with Bim, and if we cannot locate her guitar we'll take responsibility for replacing it," Roz responded. "We might ask ourselves if all this wasn't just a specific attack on Bim rather than a larger attack on the festival."

"Any attack on Bim is an attack on women's music, which she symbolizes," suggested the head of interpreting services.

"Carrie Marathon," a shuttle driver mentioned. "She and Bim are pretty much in battle gear toward each other, you know. Maybe Carrie or her friends wanted to keep Bim from performing."

"Carrie? She's a Quaker," scoffed Bluefern.

"Where in hell was Bim's Artist Care worker?" asked Roz. "Rachel? Is she here?"

"Yeah, I'm here," a most unhappy voice replied. "I can tell you, I had nothing to do with Bim's guitar being lifted. The reason I wasn't backstage was because I had a personal emergency right then. I've waited on Bim hand and foot the rest of the time, I swear!"

"We'll talk to you later." Bluefern sounded ominous, although she really didn't want to suspect Rachel. She didn't want to suspect any of the women present.

"Bluefern," said Nicky, "Let's return for a moment to the immediate practical concern of increasing security. I have a suggestion. If you assign three workers to every job, you guarantee accountability. I don't think we have *three* infiltrators in cahoots here. I think we have one angry person. She may be among us tonight. If we choose three random workers for each post, perhaps even requiring that they not know one another, we can reduce the risk of assigning our saboteur to a crucial or unsupervised job."

"That's a lot of workers, Nick, but I could manage that," Bluefern considered. "Obviously, each woman would keep an eye on the other two, while attending the task at hand. Okay, one problem is solved. For the rest of the festival, we triple security in accordance with Nicky's idea. That should keep any further mishaps from happening on stage, in the kitchen, at the gate, with the cars, with the equipment . . . What are some other at-risk spots?"

"The shuttle pool," workers called out. "Childcare. Healthcare. Communications. The performer cabins . . ."

Bluefern wrote everything down on her clipboard. "You know, we can't necessarily protect women in their cabins and tents, if theft is the big motive here. I'll get Josie to circle around some more in the morning, warning festiegoers to watch their valuables. Again, we need to bear in mind that one of us may be the culprit, may be hearing all of this info and scheming right along. Damn. I never thought it would come to this, women against women."

"Come on, Blue, with all the backstabbing and rumor-mongering that goes on in the festival community?" sneered a shuttle driver.

"No!" Roz burst out. "That's not the festival community I know. In every subculture you'll find a few bad eggs; in any gathering of several thousand lesbians you'll find a few unbalanced or vengeful women. That doesn't mean we can be undone by violence or that violent behavior characterizes a festival. Look how far we've come. Look what we've accomplished. We owe it to our festiegoers to minimize fears and maximize safety. They've all paid for the weekend, and we can still make this festival happen as planned. We want women to keep coming back. So we've lost one evening of concerts. That's happened at plenty of festivals, whether due to rain or performer illness or whatever. The show will go on. We should keep our fears to ourselves and do any, ah, detective work strictly behind the scenes."

"Excuse me, Roz. Are you saying that you don't want to make the sabotage public knowledge?" asked Bluefern, tapping her pencil on her left thumb.

"I think it's in our best interests to avoid panic."

A chorus of voices protested. "No! Everyone's got a right to know!" "That's elitist!" "This affects all of us!" "How are you going to keep things hushed up when half the festiegoers will be training as security crew?"

"I have an idea." It was Gina, coordinator of resources for Women of Color at the festival. "Bim will make sure everyone knows her guitar was stolen; that part of the news we can't hold back. And it's important to other folks on the land to be aware of a possible thief — and to know it's not a man. But when racist white women hear *thief*, they're programmed to think people of color, thanks to the media. So I want whatever info we have to be as accurate as possible . . ."

"They think *working class*, too," muttered Rachel.

". . . because I'm gonna have extra educating to do, when your white festiegoers start counting their socks and worrying about stuff being stolen. Any unfounded accusations laid on women of color and you'll all answer to me. Remember the international lesbian conference held in Switzerland in 1986? Those radical graffiti artists who spray-painted the civil defense bunkers in Geneva where conference guests had been housed free of charge? It was white women from whitest England who made that mess. But guess which women the international security forces stopped and interrogated at the borders?"

"Right on, Gina!" affirmed a number of workers.

"So what about this. Tell women about the theft, get them active as security workers. But make the story sound like the power blowout was a big accident that one thieving woman took advantage of. Don't put sabotage and infiltration into everyone's heads just yet. That's a larger political question."

"I agree with you, Gina," said Bluefern. "But we still have two problems. One is that our saboteur could be sitting right here, learning how we process, who we are, storing up insider knowledge for some future assault on women's culture . . ."

"Blue, that's a risk we take at every festival," Nicky interrupted. "We have army dykes here every summer from the base in the next county, and how do we rationalize that? Do we view them as government-funded infiltrators, spies from a violent, homophobic Pentagon? No. We view them as women who love women, who get shit for that, and who take their vacation here, at total risk to their jobs. If we start excluding women because we fear they might tell the 'wrong' people about our events or our philosophy, we sabotage outreach, networking, and accessibility."

". . . problem number two," continued Bluefern, "is that we can hardly ask the workers here, who have heard all this talk about sabotage, to take a vow of silence. I also think the performers have a right to know that they, like Bim, might be at risk, as individuals or collectively. But perhaps we can agree to talk only with each other, as necessary, about all this."

"Boy, if we lie to the festiegoers when we know there's a political problem afoot, we'll be accused of fostering elitism, perpetuating hierarchies, dressing funny, and I don't know what all," worried the young cook. "There's lots of women who say in their festival evaluation forms that they wish all festival business was discussed in the open, that they don't like the worker community being sort of separate and privileged and the festiegoers the last to know anything."

"At this point I think that a *guarded* honesty is the best policy. We beef up security, discuss only the theft issue with festiegoers, and keep looking out for a possible infiltrator —

who we encourage to come forward. Everyone got that?" Bluefern asked, looking around the circle of workers. Solemn eyes blinked back against the firelight.

"If you're here, come forward!" Gina commanded.

"We want to help you," added Roz. "Please, give us back our festival."

But no one moved to answer.

Chapter Three

All too often women think they're singing a solo in life by following
their women-identified visions.
>— Toni Armstrong Jr.,
>from *Women's Music Plus*

I'd rather be lonely than to settle for less.
>— Sue Fink,
>from "The Kind of Woman I Am"

Saturday morning on the land

Bluefern's exhausted stage crew looked up at the overcast
sky in despair.

The previous night's aborted Bim Daring concert resulted in no clear explanations for anxious festiegoers, other than Josie's assurances that a "light cable error" had created the unexpected power outage and that Bim's guitar had been stolen while no one was paying attention. Eventually, most women seemed ready to accept that statement, glad to discard the man-on-the-land theory as a wild rumor, though annoyed by the spectre of a female thief.

Melissa, an old festival hand and curious, decided to worm more information about the possible sabotage from her ex-lover on the breakfast crew.

Ceci, bruised from the crush of many hiking-booted feet, refused to leave her sleeping bag and simply slept in. Had she ventured out, she might have been surprised by the complacent attitude of many festiegoers.

Certainly, the loose wires and sudden blackout frightened and disappointed those in the Friday night audience who expected a well-run concert. But when all is said and done, lesbians do know how to amuse themselves in the dark. While Bluefern and the festival producers agonized over the ethics of procedure and precaution throughout the long night hours, hundreds of couples went back to bed and honeymooned with little complaint.

Thus to Melissa's disgust at Saturday morning breakfast, conversation focused less on the mysterious power breakdown and theft than on who had enjoyed the most orgasms after evacuation from the field.

"This sucks," Melissa complained quietly to Jen, her old lover on the kitchen crew. "We have a major crisis before us! I know, I know, I'm not supposed to think sabotage. But doesn't it occur to other festiegoers that something weird is going on? No. They're all hellbent on getting the most from their prepaid vacation. The festival could blow sky-high and half the women would merely regret that they hadn't finished their shopping in the crafts area!"

Jen, busily stirring granola, let out a sigh. "Actually, plenty of women have asked me questions, and it feels funny to downplay my own fear. The workers aren't supposed to talk too much to the festies about the problems on the land. You know, prevent general panic until we know more. A lot of public relations about how safe everyone is . . . and I wonder if that's so."

"Well, don't you think it's stupid to lie to three thousand women? Why can't we all sit in on a giant meeting and discuss what to do? I mean, it sounds like there's a nut case on the land and the workers are being told to do a massive coverup!"

Jen was pouring honey into squeeze bottles from an enormous jar. "Ah, Melissa, my feisty one. I wish we could go back to those days, when everyone identified as a worker and no one was just a guest!"

"Huh? What do you mean?"

"I mean that the festival has become *so* professional and *so* well-organized that we've distanced the audience from production. We offer a product, entertainment, for consumers, the festiegoers, who aside from their short little work shift aren't required to understand or participate in the inner workings of the festival."

She paused to tie a festival apron more sturdily around her nude brown waist. "I keep thinking about this artificial split between the workers and the festies. Are we babying the festiegoers by hiding facts from them? Or are we acting like their caregivers because they *paid* to be here?

"It's like this. You know the emergency safety regulations passengers are supposed to study on airplanes? In the unlikely event of a water landing, when you're flying from Iowa to Pennsylvania? Some passengers do watch the flight attendants' safety demonstrations, but most just doze out the window or read *People* magazine. The hope is that you won't ever be called upon to open that emergency exit door. And maintaining that hope, that it can't happen to you, or that if it does happen, there are trained professionals to rescue you, creates an illusion of security. Psychologically, you're off the hook: *Somebody else* will save your ass. In reality, you perpetuate the problem of panicky, untrained passengers by resisting the basic training that would enable you to act appropriately in a crisis."

"So, you're saying that festivals have that problem too? That women who attend just for fun assume that the security crew will take care of them instead of joining the security crew themselves?" Melissa, who had once skipped a work shift in order to have more play time at the festival, began to feel uncomfortable. She concentrated on picking up a chunk of scrambled tofu with her well-worn chopsticks.

"I'm not going to lay a guilt trip on anyone." Jen smiled. "You're always obsessed with that one time you blew off your work shift in order to seduce me."

"Stop reading my mind."

"You live with a white woman, you learn the geography of her white guilt," remarked Jen, who had grown up on a reservation. "I don't know — I'm just interested in this whole issue of who's in charge. Twenty years ago all the white lesbians I knew were living in three competing collectives near the res. They were imitating what they thought tribal culture, tribal decision-making could be. Everything by consensus, and no one really in charge. So cute — and so wrong! No one willing to see that making change requires strong leaders who can get things done, as well as group process that lasts all night.

"Any white woman who had leadership potential was thrown out of her collective for being 'male-identified,' which the women leaders in my tribe thought was crazy. Those lesbian collectives all lost their best creative people, and then they fell apart. It took a long time for white lesbians to realize that having a natural gift or a hard-earned skill didn't make one more of an oppressor, and that taking on a leadership role or showing some initiative didn't mean one was on a power trip against her sisters."

"So that means that you're okay with the festival

producers making most of the decisions, because they've done a good job keeping the festival going? You think this festival has lasted *because* of strong leadership?"

Jen paused. "I definitely trust Nicky and Roz. They've stayed true to their vision. It's the festiegoers who are less radical, complacent. I saw festival culture, when it took off in the late seventies, as a sign of white women's willingness to create a new kind of tribal culture with women of color, apart from men. And the basic respect for land usage turned me on.

"But I think festival culture changed when it added so many services that festiegoers could buy. You know there's at least two festivals where you can buy your way out of a work shift. That creates a sort of leisure-world thing, where women paying a large fee expect a resortlike experience and are less involved as planners themselves.

"And now you see" — she pointed toward a group of women who had left their used paper plates and cups in the grass — "some women now expect that 'the workers' will clean up their shit. Some women will attend festivals for ten years without ever doing any labor. Some women aren't interested in challenging their own racism. That's not a tribal culture, though we may all feel linked together as lesbians. That's an informational and spiritual split between the producers and the consumers. I'm always cleaning up white women's garbage here! I believe in being a worker. But are we creating a servant class and leisure class here? Hmm."

Melissa said nothing.

Jen covered up the granola and sat down on a hay-bale next to her.

They watched the parade of womankind stroll past. Women in pajamas, in bathrobes, in jogging shorts damp from a diligent workout; girl children squealing in proud nudity; the occasional wheelchair navigating leveled pathways.

"I've barely had breakfast and I'm already disturbed," Melissa confessed. "This whole scene, this panorama of girls, does look delightful in its variety. But you're right. Too many women are just here to party, like me before I got sober. And now there's trouble on the land and all the party girls assume that security will take care of it!"

"Bluefern and her crew are good people," Jen amended, rising to her feet again as a fresh wave of women came in to breakfast. "Their leadership is paramount. But who are the smart festiegoers who'll pick up the process, if all the leaders get injured while out on security?"

She looked over her shoulder at Melissa as she returned to work. "Look around you for one who seems out of place here, who asks too many questions, whose motives seem buried, and maybe that's the woman who's here to bring the festival down."

Out of place? Too many questions?

Melissa froze. Not — Ceci?

Back at the tent, Ceci had forced herself into a sitting position and eventually peered out the tent door. A few yards away, a woman was meditating on top of a stump. Everyone else seemed to be up and about. It was nearly elevenA.M. Ceci realized she had signed up to do her Communications work shift at noon, and, rather relieved to have an office to report to, she stood up and blew her nose forcefully. The woman on the stump looked over her shoulder, startled.

"Sorry," said Ceci.

"We're all involved in the healing process," the woman nodded agreeably.

"Huh?" inquired Ceci.

The Communications tent was jammed with workers, all doing their best to keep the question of sabotage at a discreet simmer. Overhearing their poorly concealed speculation and gossip, however, Ceci slowly pieced together a most unsettling scenario. What was afoot? A deranged festiegoer gone mad, walking among the work crews, slicing cables? An anonymous

thief pillaging from celebrity performers' gear? Two criminals
or one? Premeditated revenge or pathological acting out?

Listening to the low voices around her, Ceci felt her head
tingle with nervous perspiration. What on earth had Melissa
brought her into? Surely someone must be in charge. Surely
it was not regular protocol for a women's music festival to
confront a mysterious saboteur on the first day. Ceci looked
down at her trembling fingers and forced herself to focus on
the work sheets before her.

"Here it comes!" shouted an amused voice at four P.M.
Almost immediately, the heavens opened and it began to pour.

Later, inside their blue and white dome tent at the out-
skirts of Chem-Free and Quiet Camping, Ceci and Melissa
were unsure what to think. The sudden thundershower just
before dinner had sent them scurrying for shelter, and now
they lay side by side in mutual hunger-induced irritation,
listening to the relentless spill of raindrops on taut nylon. Ceci
leafed through a book on Jewish lesbians, munching occasionally from her plaid overnight bag of medications.

Despite the annoyance of missing the evening meal, she
was actually quite grateful to be warm and dry in her sleeping
bag, engaged in the safely familiar pastime of reading. She
flipped the pages with increasing absorption, fascinated to
learn that there were other first-generation American Jewish
women like herself attempting to build bridges between their
present lesbian urges and their complex immigrant backgrounds.

Yes, thought Ceci. I am that stereotyped creature, the
overprotected daughter of frightened immigrants. My parents
suffered unspeakable experiences in Germany: expulsion from

university, interruption of their professional work, arrest, detention, starvation, deportation to concentration camps. They worked for years before they finally made it to the United States, beginning their university careers again, re-establishing their lost credentials as professors, slowly gaining back their health and physical strength until they were able, late in life, to have a child.

Naturally, they heaped tremendous hopes and anxieties upon their one frail daughter, shielding her from both real and imagined harms in this country, nurturing her toward the educational honors they themselves prized so highly.

Ceci was never permitted to play rough games, or even to interact much with other children. Instead she spent her childhood living in the safe parentheses of scheduled activities: Hebrew school on Mondays and Wednesdays, allergy shots on Thursdays, science class at the museum, Shabbos dinner with other German survivors every Friday.

Ceci was always the smartest kid in her room at school, and was that not success? It never occurred to her parents that she might have wanted to fit in, to be "cool." "Cool" was not a legitimate achievement in their repertoire; they had suffered too much.

Despite their Orthodox backgrounds, they placed no sexist limitations on Ceci's abilities; she would be, like them, a great university professor, someday. She understood her parents' intentions, their priorities. But God, how they dressed her!

Ceci rolled over onto her back, mentally flipping through long-repressed memories as though turning the pages of a dreaded scrapbook. Look. That's me, in my corrective saddle shoes, she thought. Her first nickname was Sniffles; the next nickname, the one that lasted, was Brain. There she was on the first day of school — everyone else had a Peanuts lunchbox; she had a red plaid.

There she was at Mindy Epstein's slumber party — the

only kid whose mother picked her up before the evening was over, the only kid who didn't get to spend the night. She missed seeing *Bedknobs and Broomsticks* and making midnight fudge.

There she was in her bulky knit sweater, sitting in fifth grade, trying to ignore Mary Leigh Davis throwing spitballs at the back of my neck. All through elementary school and junior high and all through high school Mary Leigh had tormented her, calling her Brain, Dweeb, Geek, Nerd, Egghead, Weakling, Hebe, Kike, Jew-girl, and Ceci hated her. Hated her. But oh, her beautiful muscles!

Mary Leigh came to school on her brother's old hockey skates, stroking noisily into the parking lot, her strong brown calves taut and glistening. Ceci would be sitting on the steps checking her homework and Mary Leigh, her eyes flashing contempt, would hiss "Study, study, study" at Ceci.

Then she'd squirt a little Cachet on her collarbone and swish into school smelling wonderful, no one knowing she had just skated three miles to school after working out with weights in her garage-bedroom. Her parents let her move into the garage after her brother was killed, and no one in the family could bear to give away his athletic equipment.

Mary Leigh lived in that shrine to her brother, his chinning bars, his weights, his street-hockey skates, and old red sweatshirts.

One day Ceci caught Mary Leigh breaking into her locker to steal her English homework. They weren't in the same English class, but Mary Leigh had to turn in an essay by noon and she wanted to copy Ceci. Ceci came down the hall crying "What are you doing, Mary Leigh, that's my locker," and Mary Leigh grabbed her and shoved her up against the metal hardware. "Don't you think it's time some other people got the A's?" she breathed into her face. "Don't you think you've been selfish, collecting all the awards, all the scholarships, all the prizes? Huh? Don't you people ever think about spreading the wealth around?"

Even though Ceci was terrified and humiliated, it was wonderful to be so close to her. Ceci looked her straight in the eye and said, "Mary Leigh, I'll tutor you in English if you coach me for softball. I'll work with you on all your papers, all your homework, after school and weekends, if you'll coach me for softball."

Ceci smiled at the roof of the tent. For a while, it had worked. They met every other day in the park, Mary Leigh's loud disparagement of Ceci's weak muscles gradually abating in the mutual stagger toward trust.

There was the sun on Ceci's face and the unfamiliar weight of the bat and the rare compliment from Mary Leigh when Ceci actually made contact with the ball. Afterward, they occasionally shared a slice of pizza at the diner, and slowly Mary Leigh's grades improved, startling everyone in the school and bringing pride to Ceci's heart.

Then one day during park practice Mary Leigh threw a bad pitch and broke Ceci's nose. Ceci knew it was an accident, there was no malice between them any more, but Ceci's parents had gone wild, had threatened to sue, had stormed into the Davis home and presented a list of all the unflattering and anti-Semitic names Mary Leigh had called Ceci since grammar school.

Mary Leigh picked up one of her dead brother's weights and heaved it through the garage door, where it landed on the windshield of Ceci's parents' car, leaving a dent the Volvo mechanics could never repair.

Ceci, bandaged and invisible in a hospital bed, her world as shattered as the cartilage in her nose, missed softball tryouts, missed the rest of senior year, missed graduation, and spent the summer wandering ghostlike through her parents' house, making up exam work and preparing for university enrollment at MIT in the fall.

She never saw Mary Leigh again.

"Ceci?"

Melissa's voice interrupted the home movie from hell. Ceci sat up and was embarrassed to discover that thinking about Mary Leigh had created a damp place in her sleeping bag. "What?"

Melissa, beet red in the face, picked at the dried mud on her hiking boot. "Um, you know, I don't know you very well."

"No? I suppose not. Well, you know me now, I'm afraid, reluctant camper that I am. And I did tell you much of my life story during our drive from Boston." Ceci put away her bag of antihistamines with a smile. "What's up?"

"Well, listen, Ceci. I need to talk to you." Melissa looked angry, not her usual facial expression. "Women on the land need to think of all the possibilities regarding this power sabotage. I happen to know that some of the workers think a really skilled infiltrator planned the stage blackout. I'm not, like, accusing you or anything, but I've, I've learned that you're in some secret military-contract program at MIT. Damn it, I'd better be honest; I peeked at your homework while you were out taking a whiz today."

"You went through my work?" Ceci heard herself say.

"Yeah, I did. And guess what I know now: You're involved in that war games summer forum! Something you conveniently did not tell me about in the car! I can't believe a real dyke would come to a festival with, like, military-contract homework, unless she was up to no good. Ceci, you sure don't seem comfortable with or fond of the lesbian community, and you've been asking me a ton of questions about festival structures and procedures.

"I've tried getting to know you these few days and in some ways you're pretty progressive, but I also saw you over at Communications coding all those languages. CIA skills, maybe? I know you were sitting with me when the power blew, and it's not like I'm happy to accuse you of plotting something."

Melissa chewed her lip for an instant, then added, "I love this festival more than anything. I have a longer relationship with the festival than with you. So . . . if you know anything about who's tried to ruin this festival, or how it was done, I hope you'll come forward. And, naturally, I hope I'm wrong. But conscientious activists need to say these things."

Thunder.

Then, softly, the fresh heat of insult being added to injury, as Melissa's challenge swirled through the tent and landed between their faces.

Ceci spit out a Benadryl with an uncoordinated splat. "God damn it! Don't you ever accuse me of being a spy, you paranoid asshole. Don't you ever imply that I'm not lesbian enough to be trusted. Do you realize that I've taken this kind of shit my entire fucking life? Do you realize that my parents and their friends were expelled from university on suspicion of being saboteurs, nonloyal, outside infiltrators?

"Do you realize that the stereotyped image of the cunning, self-serving, untrustworthy Jew is behind most of the anti-Semitic 'precautions' taken in history? Of course I appear awkward and conspicuous at this festival, I don't have certain kinds of skills and confidence. I was never taken camping as a child. I'm in a wholly new environment surrounded by women with superior experience, and all this dust and mold makes it difficult for me to breathe.

"The last thing I'd attempt would be standing in a puddle of rainwater cutting electrical cables: That's exactly the sort of physical risk I was raised to avoid. I've spent my entire life having my intelligence used against me, as though my goals and interests as a scientist were specifically developed to alienate others rather than to cure global problems.

"I thought the lesbian community would be different, that I'd be accepted here, where the emphasis is on difference. I guess I was wrong." She leaped from her sleeping bag and began stuffing books and bananas into her plaid overnight case.

"Ceci, no! I didn't mean anything like that. Someone's made an attack on this festival, and under such circumstances we all have to ask one another hard questions. Can't you see that?" Melissa pleaded.

"Forget it, Melissa." Ceci's eyes cut around the inside of the tent like flashlight beams. "I think I'll seek out more affable quarters, perhaps in the Dweeb-Tolerant Camping Zone, where obviously you can't follow. And another thing" — she paused, one hand on the tent zipper — "I may not look like a real lesbian to you now, but by God, I'll be one by morning." Then she was gone.

For three and a half hours Ceci walked around the land in the rain, her overnight bag, slung across her chest, growing soggier and soggier. The night stage concerts were in ruins, with an overtaxed rain crew struggling to keep wires and instruments covered while drenched festiegoers sought refuge anywhere but in the open field.

Despite the sustained tension over the sabotage and the theft of Bim's guitar, however, a holiday mood prevailed in tents and cabins. For many of the women on the land, the festival represented the only vacation time in lesbian space they'd enjoy until next summer. Hoots, guffaws, and the sound of drumming poured out of damp doorways, and deep in the woods, tent walls billowed with private passions.

Eventually Ceci's rage ebbed to a slow and steady burn.

She realized she was exhausted and wet, but the prospect of returning to Melissa's tent was infinitely more uncomfortable. Lifting one foot delicately from a fern-strewn mud puddle, Ceci realized that perhaps the only way to clear her good name from suspicion was to solve the sabotage mystery herself.

She stopped in at the Community Center, where she grimly wiped out an entire contingent of Texas dykes at Trivial Pursuit in order to clear her mind for precise detail. Sipping at her reward, a hand-crafted festival mug filled with hot, sweet cocoa, Ceci leaned back in the rickety folding chair and pondered the circumstances of the missing guitar.

First of all, the few established clues all pointed to an inside job. As distasteful as this was to the loyal festiegoers and staff, someone attending the festival had planned the sabotage and stolen Bim's guitar. The important question was whether one and the same person had committed those two acts, or whether someone with a grudge against Bim had seized the opportunity of the power outage to rip off her guitar.

Ceci decided to focus on the guitar question first. From what she had heard in terms of performer gossip, Bim was beloved by many but also had a secondary reputation as a puffed prima donna who'd alienated several former friends. All factors suggested that it was not a deranged fan who had grabbed the guitar, but rather someone who had access to the stage and backstage areas, and that meant security-privileged workers or rival performers.

Of these suspects, whoever had smuggled away the guitar had not done so for purposes of economic gain. The guitar was, in fact, extremely valuable, as are all custom-made instruments, but its value lay in its workable design for Bim's needs as a left-harder. The thief would have no success reselling the guitar for much profit, and would be additionally restricted in fencing it because every women's music fan in the country would be on the lookout for the stolen goods.

Ceci closed her eyes, feeling warm hot chocolate slide down her throat. Theft without economic motive usually meant vengeance. Some woman who knew Bim's habits, had perhaps worked with her in the past, took Bim's prized possession to teach her-what? A lesson? To interrupt her tour this summer, to direct her attention away from whatever she'd planned to say at the microphone? Ha. Perhaps Bim had, indeed, planned to present controversial song material or unpopular political sentiments during her set on the night stage. Only those who worked closely with her and knew Bim's habits would know this. Carrie Marathon, perhaps?

Ceci knew a great deal more about the incident than she, as a festiegoer, was supposed to know. During her work shift at the language table in Communications, a party of Canadian performers had discussed the entire situation in French. Ceci, at the time writing translations from Hebrew to Japanese, had appeared not to be listening. In fact, however, she had understood every word, for that conversation shed curious light on Rachel.

A central suspect was Rachel Cabrini, Bim's Artist Care worker who allegedly had disappeared just before Bim's set. Rachel, subjected to unpleasant questioning later, admitted she had not been present to assist Bim backstage but insisted she'd had a personal emergency that superseded her Artist Care contract.

Bim had fumed and raged, threatening Rachel with this and that in a gross display of temper. But while Rachel had obviously been negligent in not supervising Bim's needs backstage, this was not equivalent to theft. In fact, Rachel was known to be a fond fan of Bim's and had diligently served her above and beyond the call of duty prior to the power outage.

Why, then, did Rachel refuse to provide an alibi for her whereabouts during the moment of theft? Had she something to hide? Or was the focus on Rachel a smoke screen, masking less pleasant breaches of security backstage that the festival producers were not ready to discuss?

Ceci decided to speak to Rachel herself. Although she might be weary and defensive from prior interrogations, Rachel probably held accurate impressions of the backstage working environment and personality clashes central to the entire mystery. She might speak with Ceci, a sympathetic nobody, more readily than to Bim's accusatory road crew. Feeling better, Ceci adjusted her rain gear and trod forth to Artist Care camping, where Rachel supposedly worked each evening.

Artist Care camping was an enclosed area which Ceci, a nonperformer, now saw she could not enter. She leaned against a fence post, biting her thumbnail in thought; from within her overnight bag came the rattle of medications. There! That was it! Newly empowered, Ceci marched up to the security worker on duty who wore a wet cowgirl hat covered with pins reading I LIKE SOBER DYKES and ONE DAY AT A TIME. "Excuse me," Ceci said. "I need to see Rachel Cabrini."

"I'm sorry, but if you're not a performer or a worker, I can't let you in," said the security woman. "You probably know we've had major security problems here."

"Oh, indeed," Ceci nodded vaguely. "But, you see, I'm from Healthcare. Uh, the Womb? I have Rachel's medicine — she left it behind with us by accident, and she needs it now. I'm not supposed to give it to anyone but Rachel, so, if you think you could send someone to look for her, I'll wait right here."

Ten minutes later Ceci saw the shadow of Rachel's crew cut against a cabin porch, and then Rachel herself came forward. "Listen," began Rachel, "I think there's been some mistake —"

"I'm so lucky I found you!" Ceci cut her off and gripped Rachel's arm, steering them both away from the Artist Care encampment and into a nearby Healing tent.

"I don't use chemicals," Rachel said pointedly as Ceci shone her flashlight about to make sure they were alone.

"I know. Sorry. I just wanted to talk to you, pick your

brain. Say, this tent is nice. Look at the embroidered cushions. And here: apricots!" Ceci was anxious to make Rachel feel safe.

"If this is about the whole backstage business, man, I got nothing more to say."

"I hear Bim roughed you up rather badly, with words anyway." Ceci nodded. "I'm on your side; I don't think you had anything to do with the theft or the power outage, because according to all reports you were nowhere near the night stage even though you were supposed to be waiting on Bim."

Rachel sighed. "Bim! Man, if I ever thought that Artist Care would be a cushy job, this festival has changed my mind forever. That woman is one neurotic dominatrix, and I begged in my work-exchange application to work for her. I came out to Bim's albums; I really looked forward to meeting her."

"But now you dislike her."

Rachel was no fool. "Uh-uh, counselor, you don't have motive. Sure, I've been run ragged by Bim, but nothing that would make me want to hurt her guitar. What a weird crime, anyway. No, I wasn't even there. Aw, it's too complicated to explain."

Ceci leaned forward on a cushion. "Yes, please do explain. I don't know if this will help you trust me, but my own tentmate just suggested that *I* fit the profile for a likely saboteur. Maybe I could clear both of us. So why, Rachel, did you abandon your post? Why, if you took care to ask for a specific job assignment at this festival, did you leave the backstage area just when Bim relied upon you to stand by in case she needed anything for her set? What took you away from the scene of the crime before the crime occurred?"

In spite of herself, Rachel finally smiled. "Motherhood."

"Oh! I didn't know you had a daughter in Childcare."

Rachel's smile elongated. "I don't. That's not it."

"Your partner has a little girl who needed you."

"Wrong again." Rachel's teasing tone was driving Ceci

mad; it reminded her of all the enemies she'd known in junior-high school. She tried to think of what sort of motherhood emergency would take Rachel away from work but could not be explained to the festival's pro-child producers.

Suddenly she had it.

"You don't have a daughter here. You have a son!"

Twenty minutes later Ceci was seated inside a weathered canvas tent on the far side of Mother-Daughter Camping, watching Rachel and her partner Helene change a diaper. Yes, there was no question that the olive-skinned infant, dressed in pink rompers, was, in fact, male.

"Oy, what now?" wailed Ceci, aware that she had just become privy to knowledge about illegal circumvention of festival policy.

"Come here, fofhina," Helene crooned to the baby. "Ah, he's so happy to see you again." The baby gurgled intimately at Rachel.

"So now you see the deal," Rachel sighed, sitting down cross-legged and offering Ceci a wrinkled packet of raisins. "I am a criminal, but not for the reasons they suspect. Yes, I smuggled in a boy baby! Helene and I are working dykes. We live near a resort community where there are many lesbians, many feminists, but they're mostly rich tourists, while we're the local poor brown folks who work in the hotels and in the restaurants. We end up serving the other dykes in town dinners that we ourselves couldn't afford — it's a very isolating thing, the old class system!

"One of the best things to ever happen to us was coming to this festival two years ago and going through an intensive workshop for working-class dykes. We met new friends there, women who convinced us that we could be great parents, that we didn't have to be rich to have a child."

"Yeah," Helene joined in. "So, dig this. I work in a hotel.

I knew I would be ovulating at a certain time, and I had a one-night stand with one of the better-looking hotel guests, and sure enough, I got pregnant with little Rio here."

"But, good Lord," Ceci sputtered. "Weren't you concerned about getting AIDS?"

"I know the risks, sister," Helene flashed back. "I hung around, heard things. I found out that this guy had been married for sixteen years, had just divorced, and was looking for his first-ever fling out of wedlock. He had himself tested for me when I asked him to; he was willing to postpone our date a few days, which I found pretty flattering. Yeah, he was the right guy: in very good health, and handsome. I knew his company was transferring him to London and I'd never see him again; I told him I was on the pill."

"He still could be HIV-positive and it might not have shown up yet," Ceci worried.

"We needed sperm," Rachel growled. "He passed. You think we have the dough to go to a donor bank? And among our male friends, we can't ask for donors. The men we know are very big on family line, would want a lot of control over a son. We needed to protect our independence and our own family unit."

"Well, then." Ceci's head reeled. "Why did you bring Rio to the festival? You know that not even male infants are permitted here, a rule which, I'm sure, has been challenged in the past by young mothers like yourselves."

"Yeah, because we couldn't afford to pay for childcare for a weekend and get here. We don't have friends we'd trust with our baby, nor do we wish to be separated from him. The main problem, though, is that Rio cut himself on some garden shears right before we left home, and we need to make sure we clean and dress his cut."

"The problem, you see, is that he sat on the shears," explained Helene.

"While we were all playing in the garden. He'll heal up fine, but we have to keep taking off his diaper to examine the wound, and we can't do it in front of anyone here at the festival. We must be careful to change him in the tent. The rest of the time he passes as a baby girl with no suspicion. All he does most of the time is sleep and smile at women's faces."

Ceci was beginning to get the picture. "So, Rachel, you left your post the other night because you thought something was wrong with Rio, and you couldn't have Helene bring him backstage to take off his diaper in front of others."

Rachel smiled. "Well . . . yes. And no. You see, between our work shifts and baby care, we've had no romantic time alone. Helene works in the kitchen by day, and I work in after- noons and evenings at artist's care. So the other night she sent word to me, backstage, that I should take a look at Rio, that something might be wrong, and you can bet I just up and left and ran out here to make sure everything was all right! Well, I found Rio asleep in his basket, perfectly fine. But Helene was stark naked with an incense stick and a platter of grapes, waiting for me."

Ceci blushed. The baby laughed.

"I didn't mean to make trouble for her." Helene batted her lashes. "Just some love time. I thought she'd be done working by then; I forgot about Bim's concert."

"When I got back to night stage later, much later," Rachel recalled, "everything was chaos because the power was cut. And Bim's guitar was gone. I said I'd had a personal emergency and that was all I said. I want to protect Helene and Rio from Bim's temper." She turned pleading eyes to Ceci. "You won't tell, will you?"

"No, I won't tell," Ceci promised, feeling instantly awash in guilt.

Carrie Marathon sat inside her performer's cabin, reading an old issue of *Hot Wire*. She was grateful for the privacy her quarters permitted; her road manager was off at a workshop for women's music distributors, and the cabin felt warm, hushed, still. No need to break this well-earned quiet with banjo rehearsal; Carrie was ready for her Sunday night set. But would the show, in fact, go on? Friday night's concert sabotaged; Saturday night rained out . . .

I hope the festival producers can recoup their losses, Carrie thought. Maybe I'll perform gratis, in view of the circumstances. That's sure something Bim would never do; she'll demand full pay even though she never got to sing a note.

An image of Bim, aghast and shaken at the deadly microphone, floated into Carrie's mind. No. No. Out. No more images of Bim. All the ill will she felt toward her didn't mean she wished her dead. How frightening that must have been for her! Carrie had heard that Bim threw up backstage afterward. She'd had enough humiliation, and Carrie didn't enjoy watching her suffer it, either. Ah, Bimlet. What happened to us? she wondered.

Carrie had been lying on her back, her long hair hanging off the edge of the bed and her legs upright against the cabin wall; now she swung into a sitting position and reached for her media kit. The black-and-white photos of past performances and tours went back many years, to when Carrie, a rowdy nineteen-year-old, had first burst upon the women's music scene. Bim Daring had been one of the few established star performers then, and generously shared her limelight with Carrie, inviting the younger performer to tour with her on a cross-country schedule that placed them in close quarters much of the time. Carrie adored Bim and watched her every move, imitating Bim's swaggering walk and blunt-cut mane of hair. Inevitably, they became lovers.

"I'd just like to kiss you once, Bim," Carrie had sighed over her grits one night in the North Carolina diner Bim always returned to. "Once before I die."

"Plenty of time for that, then," Bim replied, tuning her guitar.

"But, Bim," Carrie teased. "Darlin' Bim. What if I die tomorrow?" And Bim had burst out laughing and called for the bill. They walked back to their motel with poorly suppressed anticipation. Carrie remembered the incredible humidity, the smell of tobacco factories and tar and flowers heavy on the vine. Inside their motel, the Tumble Inn, Bim carefully replaced her guitar, in its handsome case, beneath the single bed they weren't going to use, and invited Carrie into the remaining double.

Carrie had made love with women before, but Bim was something else again, radiant, relaxed, powerful, emotions held just beneath her skin to trickle out at Carrie's touch. The color television in the corner, left blaring and abandoned, ran through one late-night talk show after another until finally the drone of test patterns distracted Carrie after her third orgasm. Then, too elated to sleep, they put their shorts and T-shirts back on, drove out to the river in Bim's van, and worked on songs until the sun rose. The prolonged exhilaration and lack of sleep made their next concert, later that day, a mess. But the concert after that was phenomenal. The whole rest of that tour, even more so. Carrie wondered what had become of those photographs.

She'd expurgated her press folio one angry morning, and the old pictures of tours with Bim were at home, somewhere, among Carrie's other scrapbooks and neatly boxed fan mail.

The years spent with Bim — as a lover, as a recording partner — could never be truly wiped out or even well hidden. Too many women had come out to Bim and Carrie's music, to Bim and Carrie's onstage affection and flirtation. Women's scrapbooks throughout the United States preserved photographs of the two of them together, pictures shot at other music festivals, at women's bookstores, at nightclubs and gay and lesbian Pride marches.

All of that had ended six years ago, when Carrie and Bim separated personally and professionally. Their solid reputation as folk artists had made it possible for Carrie to continue performing alone, but it was really Bim who rode the wave of her own popularity to individual star status in the women's community. And I know why, thought Carrie now, shutting the covers of her media kit with a leathery swat. Don't I just know why.

She tried to put such thoughts away. It was Saturday night, after all, at one of the best festivals in the country. Tomorrow night she'd perform on her own, flashing her banjo to the loyal crowd of followers who loved Carrie Marathon's work as much as the earlier work of Bim and Carrie. Maybe there would be a dance afterward, a fine chance to mingle, or even tingle, with somebody new. Hey, there's a good song line, thought Carrie; I should be working on new material anyhow. She reached for her Cross pen.

The cabin door wrenched open and Bim walked in. For a moment it was like every other night during their ten years together, when Carrie would be sitting cross-legged on top of the covers somewhere with her good pen and her sketchbook of songs and Bim would come back from town with a bucket of chicken and a bottle of wine. But this was a wild-haired and trembling Bim, seemingly smaller without her trademark guitar, both defenseless and crazed, her chest heaving with anger.

"I have to know, Carrie," Bim said, collapsing into a metal folding chair by the door. "Did you do it? To get even with me? Cut my power, rig my mike, steal my guitar so I couldn't play my work?"

"*Our* work," shouted Carrie, gathering up her songbook and stuffing it back into her imitation snakeskin suitcase. "No, Bim, I did not sabotage your concert. I'm not that vengeful."

"You're the only enemy I've got here, the only one who

resents me so, and you know, better than anyone, what that guitar means to me. Give it back, Carrie. Give it up to me!"

Disoriented though she was, Carrie couldn't help noticing the phrase Bim used, "Give it up to me." That had been a romantic signal, once. Now it was an accusation of theft, a hateful command. Tears spilled down Carrie's face. "I can't believe this," she managed to say. "Don't you know you already have everything valuable of mine? Why would I want your guitar in here, to remind me of that?"

"Did you bust it up? Hide it? Can I get it back, somehow?"

"Whoa. Whoa, please; look at me, Belinda Maureen. No. I did not take your guitar. I had nothing to do with the technical trouble on stage. I was actually in the audience, watching you; you can ask the other performers I was sitting with, if you don't believe me. I'm sorry I don't know what happened to your guitar." Carrie took a drink of tea from the mug at her bedside. "I can't believe you just came charging in here without knocking. What if I'd been getting it on with somebody?"

"As far as I know you're not getting it on with anybody these days; you're just sitting around feeling sorry for yourself, and blaming me. You must have just chuckled yourself silly at the sight of me on stage with no sound, no light, no set." Bim's eyes were still angry and accusing. "I have to ask you again, is there anyone else you know, like friends of yours who might be biased against me, who might sabotage my show out of some weird loyalty to you?"

"Biased! Loyalty! Jeez, Bim, why not ask if I've organized a posse? Do you really ascribe such little credibility to my following? You know, some women just like my songs: they're not coming to my concerts to spite you, to behave negatively toward you. Everything doesn't revolve around you!"

A woman in the adjacent cabin banged on the wall and

said, "Ah, excuse me, Carrie, but can you keep it down in there? Laverne's trying to meditate."

"Sorry," Carrie called back, embarrassed at being overheard.

"No problem," came the strong comedian's voice of Laverne. "Glad that you and Bim are speaking to each other again."

In the silence that followed this deadpan comment, Bim stood up and ran her fingers through stiffly gelled hair. She opened her mouth, then sat back down with a long expulsion of breath.

"Look," both of them began simultaneously.

Bim shrugged. "You first."

"No, I insist; you're the guest."

"Well, then, damn it, Carrie. Okay, you say you had nothing to do with what happened. I probably shouldn't bust in on you and lay these heavy accusations on you. I'm trying to find the guitar myself; those process queens on the security crew will never get an investigation off the ground. I'm frantic about my instrument, the rest of my tour, that's all. I didn't need for something like this to happen to me now."

Carrie, who had not exchanged words with Bim for nearly six years, was surprised now at the under-confident subtext of Bim's remarks. "What's the matter with your tour? From all accounts you're selling out, everywhere from Oakland to Binghamton."

"Yeah," sighed Bim. "I keep on going, you know, but it's —" She suddenly remembered whom she was speaking to. "Forget it. I'll go now; sorry to disturb you. Bye." She rose to leave.

"Bim, sit down," Carrie heard herself say. "Jesus, you've just been through major hell on stage. I may not like you very much, but I can't imagine how scary that would be, to come close to electrocution, to lose your old guitar. No one in women's music deserves an experience like that. Do you want some tea? Soy milk? Wait." From under a pile of underwear in the cabin bureau, Carrie produced a tiny pencil box. Inside it was a joint.

"Thanks a lot, Carrie." Bim scowled. "I'm in a program."

"Oreos, then." Fishing more thoroughly into the magic bureau drawer, Carrie pulled out a plastic bag of cookies. "Don't tell my road manager," she warned. "She's trying to keep me off sugar." They sat quietly, their mouths filled with cookies. In the cabin next door, Laverne moaned.

"Sounds like Laverne and Bev are doing more than meditating," remarked Bim.

"I was given to understand that you barfed on Laverne," Carrie pointed out. "She usually gets better reviews than that." Suddenly, they began to laugh. Bim accidentally spewed out an unfinished Oreo, and they laughed even harder. "Oh shit," gasped Carrie, red in the face and struggling for air. "Stop. I need to stay mad at you; I can't have fun with you, for Goddess' sake."

"Let go, let Goddess," answered Bim.

"You're pretty good with other people's slogans," Carrie said. "How about inventing some of your own?" For this, of course, was the real cause of the misery between them and the never-resolved breakup. Bim was a brilliant performer on stage: hearty, energetic, quick-witted with rejoinder when fans yelled seductive comments from the audience. Bim's guitar work was legendary, too; both country and classical.

But Bim was not a lyricist. She seldom wrote her own songs or performed original material, preferring to work with woman-identified ballads she'd discovered through careful research in music libraries and folklore collections. All that changed when she met Carrie, who, still fresh from a radical adolescence, had a bottomless pit of original songs and fine words to go with them.

Carrie's work was what made their joint albums meaningful as well as entertaining. But because Bim was the better-known performer, it was Bim who reaped the profits from Carrie's genius. Bim's earlier solo albums continued to sell as her reputation improved, and Bim and Carrie's successful tours had financed Bim's *Greatest Hits* — an album containing four of Carrie's best songs.

Poorly compensated, lacking the capital and the confidence to strike out on her own, Carrie suffered through another year or two of serving as Bim's ghost writer. Finally she demanded her share of the profits, threatening to spill the beans in the pages of *Lesbian Connection*. In the ensuing ugly scenes of accusation and cross-accusation, their relationship crumbled, as messily irreparable as the cookies they now ate instead of each other.

"You've run out," said Carrie.

"Huh?"

"Of material. That's what you meant, when you said you didn't need something like this to happen now. With your guitar in hand, you can still do the instrumental hits, improve on them, or reinterpret them. Losing your guitar just reinforces your sense of exposure. You don't have any of your own songs to sing."

"Thanks, Dr. Freud," Bim replied, brushing Oreo crumbs from the knees of her jeans. She rested her head between her large hands, a gesture Carrie remembered and still found to be a turnon.

"You know that's why I'm angry with you, because you got all the credit and I was assumed to be a sidekick rather than a songwriter."

"I know," Bim admitted.

"I found your lack of integrity appalling, and I split. But, Bim, if I really wanted to, uh, get even, as you say, I would have gone to someone in the women's music press and testified against you in excruciating detail. I didn't. Because I didn't want *our* albums tied up in litigation and another women's music label plowed under through artist in-fighting.

65

That, to me, is the real sabotage. I didn't want that to happen to us."

"To us?" asked Bim, lifting her head.

"Well, to the community, to women's music, to me. Even if I felt you offered me insufficient credit and money, I shut up about it because I was so thrilled at hearing my songs in women's cafés and bars. I didn't want women to think, when they heard my songs, "Oh, that's the song that's causing all the controversy between Carrie Marathon and Bim Daring.' I wanted to just take the money you offered and go, strike out on my own, because by then I was ready."

Bim looked at her with mingled irritation and respect, an expression that oddly suited her strong features. "Well, you've won, sweet pea. 'Cause I've run out of material and you're headlining all over the East Coast. Your stuff gets better and better. You think I don't hear it? Sure I buy your tapes. But I can't imitate them. Your style's changed; it's grown older. Older than me."

Carrie looked down at her lap.

"Guess I really should go now," Bim said.

"Wait," Carrie interrupted. "Since we're finally talking, I have to ask you something. This isn't easy for me to — Whew. Okay. Bim, a couple of years ago I had a lump removed from my breast. I thought I had cancer, and it was very scary until the tests proved everything was benign. Anyway, the procedures were pretty expensive, and some of my friends held a benefit concert while I was in the hospital. They raised a substantial amount of money for me, far more than I would have thought possible from the ticket prices they charged.

"It turned out that some anonymous woman donated several thousand dollars, and I never knew who that was. I figured it was a love-struck fan of substantial means, or someone who supported women's music causes." She paused, her hair now hiding her face.

"Bim," she asked in her quietest voice, "Was it you?" The

cabin walls, warped from years of rains, creaked ever so slightly.

"Yes," said Bim.

"Then come here," Carrie Marathon said, opening her arms. Together again.

Chapter Four

After the Israelites cross the Red Sea, Miriam leads the women in a
dance. And to me, this is kind of an amazing thing. Here's this
movement. Being liberated, going through the process of liberation
out in this total wilderness, and they're dancing! And to me that
really is an incredible symbol of how we need to celebrate every step
along the way, and not just look at the end as being the only thing
that's important. Each step in the process of liberation is important.
> — Laura Berkson,
> at Campfest

Be still my beating heart and lower.
> — Maxine Feldman,
> at the East Coast Lesbian Festival

Fierce downpours continued, and the festival rain crew simply wrapped the night stage in waterproof tarps and moved a few of the acoustic performers into the dining hall for an abbreviated, makeshift show. Ceci heard laughter and cowgirl whoops as she trudged back from her clandestine introduction to Rachel and Helene's baby.

The crowded dining hall bulged with womankind. At one end, a huge stone fireplace was well utilized: dangling over the blazing logs were dozens of pairs of wet socks. The food tables had been pushed back to accommodate rows of folding chairs, and Ceci peered through a sea of multicolored breasts and interesting haircuts, hoping in vain to locate a seat. Two lesbian comedians, perched on barrels at the front of the hall, teased and sassed their captive, rain-soaked audience.

"What's the real reason lesbians have short fingernails?" asked performer number one.

"Ha!" shouted the crowd.

"Because no one had any fingernails left after years of attempting to open those discreetly stapled issues of *Lesbian Connection*," said performer number two.

All around Ceci were women kissing, women touching one another's bare limbs, women wringing out wet clothes and applauding the entertainment with bare-assed, unself-conscious approval. Steam rose in a warm, sweet cloud from the toasting socks, the drying hair of three hundred heads, the bodies pressed close together in patchouli harmony.

Am I the only one here without a date? Ceci wondered miserably. Sitting cross-legged inside a watermelon crate, she fished through her overnight bag for an aspirin and caught sight of her new book about Jewish women. Hypnotized by reading material under any circumstances, Ceci opened the book and resumed reading the chapter she had nearly finished before leaving Melissa's tent.

"Don't tell me you're reading a book here," laughed the woman nearest to Ceci, who wore sneakers and a tool belt. "Live a little, girlfriend!"

"I love reading," Ceci replied, feeling defensive.

"I love women," Tool Belt replied, returning her gaze to the two comic performers. "Only live once, kid!"

Ceci scrambled to her feet, splintering the watermelon crate into fifteen pieces. That's it. I'm out of here, she thought grimly, her wet feet slapping flipperlike toward the exit. Why can't I just be myself? What is this elusive and mystical lesbian ideal one is expected to conform to?

She began to sob, and, half walking and half running now, plunged out of the dining hall and down the hill, toward the circle of dorm-style cabins where some festiegoers stayed. I'll just sit here for a moment and bawl, Ceci told herself, ducking into the shelter of a cabin porch. She sat down with a defeated slump, letting the familiar player piano of self-pity roll out its notes inside her head.

One: I'm not an athlete; I'm skinny and pale, burn easily in the sun, carry around an inhaler, have no muscles to speak of, no wind, no history of team jollity or skill; I never made softball, can't shoot pool, don't lift weights, can't seem to learn the country-and-western two-step.

Two: I would rather read than drink beer, a choice every American television commercial and pop-cultural norm suggests is impossibly aberrant and subversive.

Three: I have no sexual experience beyond the realm of fantasy and self-exploration, have never kissed another woman, have never made the first move; I lack the romantic and physical frame of reference most of these women take for granted.

Four: In the religious Jewish communities I call home, scholarship and mental acuity, rather than athletic or sexual prowess, are the hallmarks of honor, but only if one is male; a brainy daughter is expected, at some point, to put away her texts and become a wife and mother. I am suspect in my ethnic group because I am female.

I am suspect in lesbian culture because I am academic. I'm even suspect within academia, at MIT, because I support gay and Jewish causes. There's no hope for me. I'm a terminal outsider. And the outsider is not welcome.

Ceci's muffled sobs had alerted someone inside the cabin. The screen door opened, and a woman's voice called out, "Well, hey, there. Why weren't you at havdala? What are you doing sitting wet and alone in the cold night air?" It was Trudy, the woman Ceci had met while waiting in line for her shower Friday evening. Trudy, who had pulled Ceci away from the shower and into the woods for wild Sabbath dancing.

"It's you!" Ceci managed to say.

"You were expecting maybe Barbra Streisand? Did you come looking for me or what? You don't look so good. I mean that as a compliment, you understand; yesterday you were quasi-radiant."

"Oy," Ceci chuckled, blowing her nose. "That's the nicest thing anyone's said to me so far. I'm on your porch by accident; I was feeling sorry for myself and needed a solitary corner."

"What's the matter? Someone hurt your feelings? Listen, one minute. One minute. I have some treats in my backpack. A little snack might cheer you up. Hang on." She ducked back inside the cabin.

I must look hideous, Ceci thought. How incredible that I happened to end up outside of Trudy's cabin. I wished myself right into Jewish lesbian space! Perhaps this book has magical properties, she told herself, fingering the text on Jewish lesbian identity.

Trudy returned to the porch steps with a blanket and two bags of miniature chocolate bars. "They're kosher," she assured Ceci, who was hastily scanning the fine-printed ingredients.

"It's peanuts I'm allergic to," Ceci explained. "But these chocolates are fine. And tasty. How absolutely wonderful; thank you so much!"

"L'chayim," laughed Trudy. "S'iz gornisht." It's nothing.

"It is so something. And you speak Yiddish. I was really intrigued by the Hebrew you used yesterday; I'd never heard those prayers recited in the feminine before. Languages fascinate me, although my research field is physics. To be honest, I've been feeling pretty isolated at this festival; much of lesbian political culture is new to me. Or, rather, I've appreciated it through books rather than experience, and I'm regrettably unprepared for this large-scale embodiment of alternative community."

Trudy nodded her head. "Everyone suffers from festival syndrome on occasion. I went to an Alix Dobkin workshop last winter; she's a Jewish lesbian folksinger and has been a festival worker for years. She pointed out that part of being at a festival includes being frustrated and miserable, because our ideals are being tested. We create the matriarchy here, bit by bit, and there's no perfect blueprint for that. We know what we don't want, and are often critical of one another as a result. It can be stressful, this lesbian holiday!"

"And, of course, the question of sabotage hardly eases festival stress," Ceci admitted. "I assume you know that there's more going on here than the theft of a guitar. You're a worker, right?"

"Yeah, I'm backup staff for Healthcare. I do know about the sabotage attempt, and boy, I have labored strenuously to keep quiet about it, too, since my natural instinct is to warn women of all possible danger factors in their environment. But this year I'm really at the festival for my own pleasure, and that's why I reserved a space in this comparatively luxurious festiegoer cabin. A real mattress, for once, instead of my ever-leaking tent. You know, some festivals you approach as a righteous worker, some you approach as private healing time, depending on where you're at — well, I guess you don't know."

"So tell me about it, then," Ceci suggested, through a mouthful of chocolate.

Trudy wrapped the blanket around their shoulders and gave a preliminary chuckle. "Well, sister, I'll give you a sense of festival history, or herstory, and I must say the sight of you eating chocolate does take me back to my very first festival. It was . . . hmm, I'm giving away my age here . . . nineteen eighty-three, and I was twenty-three."

"I'm a little older than that now," said Ceci.

"Well, back then, when I started out, women's music festivals were still in their infancy to some degree. Certainly they were less sophisticated and with far fewer comforts, except for those festivals meeting on university campuses. (Where you can't take off your clothes, doll; alas.) Okay, there I was, just finished college, but already as out as the backyard, and just aching for an eyeful of women's bosoms; I'd seen my lesbian friends' photos of this festival!

"The festiegoers in our town rented a tour bus and driver to take us here, and the trip was at least twenty hours long. Everyone on the bus was in a couple except me, so I had to take the one single seat in the rear by the rest room. All throughout the trip, women stumbled by my head to pee, and eventually two women tried to smoke a joint in there and received a stern lecture from our driver about 'foreign tobaccos.'

"We pulled into some truck stop for breakfast after a long night on the road, and just picture sixty dykes pouring into the restaurant for coffee and eggs. We completely took over the bathroom, too, washing our faces, brushing our teeth, changing clothes, buying tampons. The regular patrons were absolutely aghast.

"One trucker asked if we were on our way to a Girl Scout reunion. Other folks just stared. 'I was a Girl Scout,' bellowed

73

a six-foot black woman from our group; 'Until they threw me out!' She let out this great, well-satisfied laugh.

"Then the woman with her, carrying a duffel bag painted with goddess symbols, added 'I was a Camp Fire Girl,' and additional voices chimed in up and down the line until rival teams of women were shouting 'Girl Scouts!' and 'Camp Fire Girls!' We had a fake fight with those tiny packets of imitation maple syrup, and then licked it off each other.

"I'm almost positive I had a dyke waitress: She wouldn't take my money, told me to save it for festival souvenirs. Apparently there had been caravans of festiegoers through there before."

"It is funny," admitted Ceci. "The woman who gave me a ride here, Melissa, posted an enormous sign in one of her car windows, informing all and sundry that we were festival bound or bust. I felt all eyes on us even as we drove. Yet the other women on the road bound for this place did notice us and wave, or honked their horns."

"That's part of the fun. So, let's see. I had packed plenty of gear and was well equipped to camp and withstand rain or heat or insect attacks. But I wasn't prepared for the dreariness of the food! Back then, we didn't get nice thick veggie-burritos with chili, or lasagna with sour cream and cheese, or any of the amazing soups-for-three-thousand you now enjoy here. No, we had boiled gray potatoes with yogurt dip three times a day, livened up with the occasional sad carrot.

"Women were flinging themselves into the Porta-Janes. And there were no concessions operations selling munchies and ice cream and tea, or meat barbecue, on the side, though now that's a big source of festival income. The only snack for purchase was popcorn, which you had to call 'momcorn.'

"Had I grasped the situation beforehand I would have packed a muffin at least, some minty tea bags, some Ding-Dongs. So, anyway, to make a long story short, well, I cruised a woman for no other reason than her possession of a giant bag of M&M's. I was desperate!"

"What happened?"" Ceci was curious.

"Oh, we laughed and talked and ate M&M's all night long. It was fun. In fact, we wrote to each other for a while. Heh. Plenty of amusing things happened at my first festival. I was lying down in the day stage field, wearing sunglasses and nothing else, and some babe swooped down on me and gave me a long lip kiss. When I sat up and took off my shades, the poor lady gasped, 'Oh. You're not Clare!' and took off in mortification."

They laughed together.

"So . . . now you're laughing rather than crying," Trudy observed with satisfaction. "What's on your mind?"

"Oy, my mind, my mind," sighed Ceci. "My mind is on my mind. I'm a graduate student at MIT, and the friend who drove me here, whose tent I'm sharing, vaguely suspects me of masterminding the sabotage. At least she feels comfortable in holding up my brainy-girl awkwardness as proof of collusion with things unlesbian. I stormed out of our tent, soaking my head nicely, and I simply don't know where to go tonight: It seems I'll never fit in here, in this rowdy good-old-girl culture. I just want peace and quiet."

"You can sleep in our cabin, doc. I was just about to turn in myself." Trudy stood up and stretched. "I have a spare sleeping bag you can use."

"Oh . . . no, n-no," Ceci stammered, feeling the back of her neck heat up like a boarding-house hot plate. "I didn't mean to fish for accommodations." She looked longingly at the interior of Trudy's cabin, where women were turning out lights, climbing quietly into their separate bunks, and wishing one another sweet dreams.

"You want to catch a cold, wandering around wet and miserable like that? Come on. We're safe. *I'm* safe. Indulge yourself; spend a night on a bed, under a wood roof."

This offer was simply too tempting for Ceci to decline, although she wondered if Melissa might be looking for her. Trudy scooped up Ceci's damp gear and what remained of their chocolate feast and tiptoed back into the cabin, smiling broadly; although Ceci didn't notice in the dark.

"Are you sure you all don't mind my sleeping here? I mean," Ceci whispered, "I haven't paid for cabin space. I didn't even know it was an option. I'm supposed to be up in Chem-Free." From the bunks around them came the soft breathing and assorted snorts of sleeping lesbians, sounds Ceci had become accustomed to from camping in the woods. An occasional syllable of dream-babble floated down to them from an upper bunk.

"What's to mind? There's an extra space because one woman left. No problem." Trudy moved the two iron bed frames in the corner closer together so they could whisper without disturbing their sleeping cabin-mates.

"Here, bubeleh, put this on." She handed Ceci a warm flannel nightshirt.

Ceci stretched out gratefully on the soft mattress. It was wonderful to be in something resembling a real bed after being kicked about in the mob stampede and then sleeping on hard, rooted ground. She felt her body relax for the first time in days and let out an involuntary moan.

"Is this your first camping experience?" Trudy asked quietly. "It must be a rather overwhelming time for you."

Ceci sighed. "Yes. I've had very little outdoor experience, and I certainly never went camping as a kid. The woods hold all sorts of terrors for my parents, who probably participated in scouting activities themselves as kids but later came to know the German forests as unfriendly labyrinths while they were being pursued by Nazis." She shuddered at this image.

"I'm sorry that the facts of my upbringing invoke such melodrama."

"Your parents are survivors?"

"Yeah."

"Mine too."

"You're kidding!" Ceci leaned up on elbow, astonished.

"Sure. It's not unusual to find daughters of survivors at lesbian festivals, by the way; there's probably other women like us here as well. We should do a workshop next year. Let's see. Okay, my mother grew up in Poland, and during the war she was taken in by some sympathetic Catholic nurses and hidden in a hospital bed for months. It made a deep impression on her, she tried for years to convince me to become a nurse. Apparently, that hospital was a center of resistance activity, with the nuns using drugs to bribe authorities. A lot of the nuns and nurses were executed over time."

"Did you become a nurse?" Ceci whispered.

"No, I drive an ambulance. Same thrill of saving lives, but I get to wear dykier clothes and map out traffic routes. I did nursing school for a while and then switched to paramedic training. I know what you mean about having overprotective parents. My mother's chief concern about my lesbianism, for instance, is that I've *chosen* an endangered cultural identity, while her Jewishness was something she inherited. She doesn't see sexual orientation as innate. She doesn't see the connection, that lesbian identity, like our Jewish roots, creates a will to survive against odds, an ability to live as outsiders and insiders in the fight for justice. I'm sure she chiefly wants to spare me from the sorts of social persecutions she saw in her youth."

"Are you, uh, out to her?" Ceci wanted to know.

"Kinda sorta. We've become closer since my father died. I should have mentioned that he was in a concentration camp for eight months before liberation. He met my mother at a survivors' picnic in Los Angeles in the fifties. Anyway, back to the present. My mother has met several of my partners in the past and seemed friendly to them all, fed them large quantities of kugel anyway. I'm, um, not with anybody now." This last remark seemed to hang in the air.

Good God, thought Ceci. Here I've stumbled into the cabin of the one woman on the land who knows exactly what I'm all about and I am hopeless, hopeless. I want to say or do something, and I cannot move. I am utterly incapable of turning this situation to my advantage. Why must my mind be so much more articulate than my body? Look at her: She is wonderful, handsome, strong. I've got to touch her or I will implode with longing, like an atom, and there is no privacy, there are women sleeping all around us! Ceci flinched involuntarily as Trudy's elbow brushed against her.

"Man, you're really tense, girlchik. Would you like a backrub?"

The oldest line in the book, thought Ceci. Or so everyone says. What do I know? When have I lived? Aloud she said, "Sure."

"Don't worry," whispered Trudy, shifting their two beds together to form one large square and rolling up the sleeves of her well-faded Olivia Records sweatshirt. "I'm very good at this. CPR training, nursing school, you know." She deftly turned Ceci onto her stomach and began kneading her back and neck muscles with warm, skilled hands.

"Ohh," said Ceci.

"Shh," laughed Trudy. "This doesn't hurt? This feels all right?"

"Yes," Ceci responded, desire slowly gathering in the pit of her stomach and pleasantly pinwheeling outward from there. She breathed dizzily into the pillow, glad to be at least temporarily spared an allergy attack by the alien flannel.

"You have beautiful bones, nice bones." Trudy worked seriously, moving her palms with competent pressure around Ceci's ribs and shoulder blades. In the darkness the only sounds were women breathing and skin on skin. Outside, rain dripped sensuously from tree branch to tree branch.

Abruptly Ceci rolled over and pulled Trudy down on top of her. For a moment neither of them spoke. Then Trudy whispered, "Are you sure this is what you want?"

"I want," said Ceci, wrapping her leg over Trudy's, astonished at her own bravado.

"How quiet can you be?" whispered Trudy.

"I don't know," answered Ceci, her fingernails pulsing. "I've never done this before."

Trudy slowly lowered her mouth onto Ceci's in the dark. The bedsprings squeaked approvingly.

"Shit," gasped Ceci. She glanced wildly around at the bunks filled with sleeping women. "I'm sorry. Oy, don't stop. I'll really try to be quiet!"

Trudy smiled, her white teeth gleaming. "No problem, doc. Just keep your tongue in my mouth."

Outside, the rain gradually slowed to drizzle, then to a fine mist. Animals emerged from their burrows, sniffing the air, eager for a few hours of night foraging after the prolonged storm.

Melissa worriedly kept a Coleman lantern shining in case of Ceci's return.

Down by the shuttle stop, three dykes in orange security vests sat around a campfire, laughing and eating badly squashed Twinkies.

And deep, deep in the woods, another woman sat alone on a log, shivering and looking at a knife.

Inside the cabin, the temperature had risen several degrees.

Trudy had zipped their two sleeping bags together, so that she and Ceci lay in a private cocoon sack of warmth. Ceci found herself naked against Trudy's bare hipbone. They both sighed at the mutual contact of warm skin.

"Oh my God," whispered Ceci.

"Shah, shah," soothed Trudy into Ceci's breasts. "Listen. All around us, hear the sleep of fellow passengers, our sisters on this journey. Deep in the belly of this ship we all sail toward America. There will be women's land there, safety and warm dances."

"Yes," Ceci heard herself repeating over and over.

Trudy's hand cupped the back of Ceci's head and kneaded the tense little muscles there, then brought Ceci's face toward her own again.

As quiet as a pond, they exchanged tongues, feeling the tiny soft hairs at the corners of their mouths.

"A shayne maidel," Trudy exulted, and entwined her toes with Ceci's.

"Oh, please, speak to me in Yiddish again. It's so wonderful, that you know these words. They're my words, my language."

"Du macht a loch in hartzen, shvester; you make pain in my heart, my sister, from your loneliness. Shah. Into my bed you have come, my sister, my bride."

"That's the Song of Songs," Ceci remembered. "Say it to me. All of it. The whole Hebrew scripture, as much as you know."

"O that you would kiss me with the kisses of your mouth, for your love is better than wine."

"Yes," gasped Ceci.

"Ani l'dodi v'l'dodi li. I am my beloved and my beloved is mine. My beloved is unto me as a bag of myrrh that lieth between my breasts. My beloved is unto me as a cluster of henna in the vineyards of Ein Gedi. Behold, thou art fair, my love; behold, thou art fair; thine eyes are as doves."

"More," demanded Ceci, running her fingers through Trudy's hair.

"Behold, thou art fair, my love, and pleasant; our couch is leafy, the beams of our houses are cedars. I adjure you, O daughters of Jerusalem, by the gazelles, and by the hinds of the field, that ye awaken not, nor stir up love, until it please."

"It pleases me," Ceci affirmed, breathing unevenly. Steam had begun to gather on the cabin window. Trudy slid down in the bed, her tongue writing the passages of poetry across Ceci's erect nipples.

"Rise up, my love, my fair one, and come away; for, lo, the winter is past, the rain is over and gone, the flowers appear on the earth; the time of singing has come, and the voice of the turtle is heard in our land."

"Slower," gasped Ceci, watching Trudy's head gradually disappear between her legs.

"Thy two breasts are like two fawns that are twins of a gazelle, which feed among the lilies. Come with me from Lebanon, my bride; thou hast ravished my heart, my sister, my bride; thy lips, O my bride, drop honey; honey and milk are under thy tongue."

"Slower."

Then, for a long time, no words, only motions and reaction. Desire, longing, too much, shy, shy, start over. Keep going. Trudy resurfaced and curled against Ceci's body, stretching warm fingers down to where her tongue had played.

"I sleep, but my heart waketh," whispered Ceci.

"Open to me, my sister, my love, my dove, my undefiled; for my head is filled with dew, my locks with the drops of the night."

"Yes," moaned Ceci, her thighs trembling. "I rose up to open to my beloved; and my hands dropped with myrrh, and my fingers with flowing myrrh. I opened to my beloved."

"This is my beloved, and this is my friend, O daughters of Jerusalem," wrote Trudy's tongue on the back of Ceci's neck.

"Don't stop."

"The roundings of thy thighs are like the links of a chain; thy navel is like a round goblet, wherein no mingled wine is wanting; thy belly is like a heap of wheat set about with lilies; thy neck is as a tower of ivory; thy nose is like the tower of Lebanon."

"I broke it in twelfth grade," Ceci gasped.

"I will climb up into the palm tree; I will take hold of the branches thereof; and let thy breasts be as clusters of the vine, and the smell of thy countenance like apples; and the roof of thy mouth like the best wine, that glideth down smoothly for my beloved, moving gently the lips of those that are asleep."

"Amen," from Ceci.

"Set me as a seal upon thy heart, as a seal upon thine arm; for love is as strong as death; many waters cannot quench love, neither can the floods drown it."

"Kdosh, kdosh, kdosh," responded Ceci. "Holy, holy, holy. Keep going, keep going, don't stop."

"My heart overfloweth with a goodly matter; my tongue is the pen of a ready writer," recited Trudy.

"It sure is," Ceci breathed. "Hebrew school was never like this.

"And Ruth said: entreat me not to leave me, and to return from following after thee."

"For whither thou goest, I will go."

"And where thou lodgest, I will lodge. Thy people shall be my people."

"Slower. Slo-o-wer."

"And Miriam took a timbrel in her hand, and all the women went out after her with timbrels and with dances, and Miriam sang unto them."

"Because she was the prophetess; the sister of Moses."

"Come into the Red Sea, then, with me, now. We're crossing it, you and I, now. Hear it trembling on either side of us? No waters close over our heads. We rush through, alive, now."

Ceci heard the crush of parted water, the beckoning desert beyond both hard and hopeful. She saw, on that far side, Trudy, dressed as Miriam, dancing with music, in brown bare feet. She felt her entire skin begin to tingle, a sensation so intense it had a color all its own.

"Keep going. Keep going — oh!"

In the early morning, Ceci woke up feeling like a million bucks. When her eyes had focused she discovered she was lying naked on top of Trudy. Trudy's Star of David necklace, on its long beaded chain, had come apart during the previous night's liveliness. Trudy lay peacefully sleeping with dozens of tiny rainbow-colored beads scattered around her limbs.

Girlfriend, thought Ceci, trying out the word inside her head. Lover.

"Mmm," sighed Trudy.

Cautiously, Ceci lifted her head and craned her neck to see if any of their cabin-mates were awake yet. She noticed that several other women had paired off during the night, or were, at least, sleeping two to a bed. Perhaps the whole cabin, then, had been surreptitiously at play, each couple caressing secretly at the lowest possible decibel, no one wanting to disturb or alert the other bunks. The cabin walls did have a peculiarly rosy glow. We're all asleep inside a giant vulva, thought Ceci, and then realized that the rare-colored light was simply sunrise coming through the windowpanes.

"Hi," said Trudy, kissing Ceci's nose.

"Hello," Ceci whispered back. "Look at the light on the walls."

"Cool," breathed Trudy. "Let's go watch the sun come up down at the lake."

"There's a lake here? I didn't know that — oh, gevalt! I don't have any dry clothes to put on."

Trudy sat up, wrapping warm arms and a bathrobe around

Ceci. I love you, thought Ceci, in a moment of brilliant clarity. Was I all right last night? Did I make an idiot of myself? Do I look different today, I wonder . . . What if I never see you again after the festival . . .

"You're thinking and worrying again." Trudy nudged her. "Be happy. Come on, let's go look. The lake is beautiful; we'll have it all to ourselves."

Quietly they laced on their sneakers and picked up their cameras. Trudy strode confidently out the door wearing nothing but surfing jams and her Minolta camera.

"Aren't you cold?" asked Ceci, floundering in Trudy's giant bathrobe. Look at her gorgeous breasts, she thought wildly.

"No, now that it's stopped raining the air feels great. I'm used to getting up early and running a few miles at the fire station anyway. Hey, you look cute as hell. Anyone ever tell you that?"

"Just you."

"And rightly so."

They encountered one of their cabin-mates on the porch, going through tai chi motions. The woman paused to smile knowingly at Ceci.

"I, um, hope we didn't keep you awake last night," Ceci stuttered, casting about for the proper etiquette in this situation.

"Well," the wiry black woman replied thoughtfully, "it wasn't the moaning so much. That was rhythmic; I fell asleep to it. It was the eventual bursts of laughter that threw me off!"

Mortified, Ceci scurried away, while Trudy burst with laughter one more time.

They followed a rough trail through the woods to a more pebbly and sloping road. Ceci, who had not seen much of the land beyond her own camping spot and the central event areas, looked about her with interest as they passed the Sober Support tent, a video tent, an impossibly muddied softball diamond, and two children's wading pools. One of these had apparently been turned into a sex tub for grownups; extinguished red candles, several black bras, and a lavender latex glove were floating on top of murky rainwater.

"There's something for everyone here," she remarked.

"Some*one* for everyone, too," Trudy amended, slipping her hand into Ceci's.

The festival grounds were far more extensive than Ceci had thought. Eventually she caught sight of the distant glimmer of water framed by dark green foliage. A rutted trail, covered with pine boards to accommodate wheelchairs, led through the trees, and suddenly they were on a reedy beach, the clearing opening up like cupped hands. The lake lapped around a weathered wooden dock. From green hills on the far side, orange clouds parted and the light of sunrise filled up the natural bowl of water and land.

Everything was mist-hushed, damp and glowing.

"Incredible," said Ceci. "I'm so glad you kicked me out of bed to see this."

"Because you are a rose of Sharon," Trudy murmured. "A lily of the valley."

"Don't start with me again unless you're going to finish," Ceci was amazed to hear herself say. In answer, Trudy pulled Ceci into a wide canoe bobbing just below the dock, and with one broad foot pushed away.

"Are we allowed to use the canoes?" Ceci asked nervously.

"We are now," Trudy responded, her hands on Ceci's hair. They kissed, rocking on the water.

"God, you make me feel so good; I can't believe I'm out here in a canoe, in the middle of a lake with you."

"Last night we pretended we were in a ship, sailing to safe shores," Trudy said. "Let's continue the metaphor, shall we?"

"Metaphors of ships and compasses. And I want to sail, sail, and never drop anchor," Ceci whispered into Trudy's ear.

Gently, delicately, they made love in the canoe.

Eventually the sun emerged in full, shining strong heat down upon their bodies. Birds and cicadas blared mightily in the woods around the lake. Ceci sat up, her neck covered in hickeys. "Look how far we've drifted!"

"Well, no problem," Trudy smiled, goosing Ceci with the oar they had hurled aside. "Are you hungry? Do you need to go back? Or can we paddle to the other side just to see it? I've always wanted to see it. We're almost there anyway."

Ceci thought briefly of Melissa, who was probably worried about her or even looking for her. "No, no," she said. "I want to keep drifting with you, please."

Trudy paddled with incredible energy and skill, water and storm-tossed blossoms dripping from her oar. Ceci, seated tentatively in the stern of the canoe, gave up matching Trudy's pace and simply rowed at a more moderate speed. "We're not in the head of the Charles regatta, here," she gasped.

"Sorry, babe," called Trudy over her shoulder. "I love a good workout. Did you ever row crew, at MIT?"

"Me? N-no," Ceci panicked, frantically flipping through her mental Rolodex in a search of a credible athletic history. "I wanted to play softball in high school, but it, it didn't work out. That's when I had my nose broken."

"That must have hurt like hell," winced Trudy.

"It did, indeed. Oy vey, I can hear it now, the sound of the ball hitting my face, when she pitched it at me too hard."

"She?" inquired Trudy, turning to wink at Ceci.

"It's nothing like that. Or, rather, it was something like that. I did like her, but just when we began to be friends this accident happened at practice. My parents had a fit, really lost all reason and dignity, and there were several ugly confrontations. It was the end of my friendship with Mary Leigh, and certainly the end of my softball career." Ceci felt her eyes well up involuntarily, whether from the memory of the ball hitting her nose or from the memory of Mary Leigh, she wasn't sure. She was glad Trudy could not see her face.

"I rowed crew in college, which my mother could not understand," Trudy reminisced. "It was too WASP, too preppy. Primarily, though, she was afraid I would drown."

"My parents were afraid I'd get hurt in every arena of physical exertion," Ceci growled. "It's remarkable that I got beyond hopscotch. Unfortunately, I was sick a lot as a kid. I'm not particularly, um, butch now either."

"You're doing fine," Trudy encouraged her. "Running around the land all night, wild sex until dawn, then out for a brisk walk and an erotic canoe race, and no allergy attacks so far."

"One tends to feel safe with a paramedic," Ceci agreed shyly. They had reached the far side of the lake, which resembled their own festival grounds with a battered pier and small beach area. Probably another summer camp facility, thought Ceci. I wonder if anyone's there.

"Don't worry. No one's staying over here," Trudy announced, reading Ceci's mind. "It's gone unrented for years. If this camp was in session we'd all be told to wear bathing suits in the lake, in case these other campers went out on their dock and saw us."

Ceci jumped out of the canoe and helped Trudy pull it to shore. "So how do you know nobody's here?" she asked.

"I told you, the festival producers would inform everyone in advance if they knew there were men or boys in the area. This camp's been abandoned for two years, I think. They had some kind of fire. I was here that summer, and we saw the smoke rising across the lake. Luckily, no one was hurt; they got the kids out in time." Trudy turned around. "Ceci?"

Ceci stood rooted to the sand, every mark of love-making and sunburn glaring red against her skin, her mouth open in unvoiced fear as she traced the jagged graffiti carved into the dock: WHITE POWER. Below it was a swastika.

"Hell's bells," Trudy breathed.

"It's everywhere, isn't it?" said Ceci in a dead, flattened tone, her toes curling inside her soaked sneakers. "Even at a lake, such a beautiful place, it follows us. This hatred."

"It must have been some kids, some camper assholes, or local vandals," Trudy spoke angrily, and held Ceci close to her. "So much for visions of sailing to Ein Gedi. We should have stayed in bed."

"I don't know, Trudy. This carving looks pretty fresh to me. See the white splinters? God, it makes me feel creepy; let's get the hell out of here. And let's tell the festival producers about this. Women shouldn't canoe over here alone."

"Ah, Ceci," Trudy said with sudden dismay, "I think someone already has." She pointed to a thickly rooted tree a few yards up the beach. Someone else had pulled a smaller canoe up to its base — a canoe loaded with camping supplies, food, and other survival equipment.

Their skins chilled with apprehension. Ceci and Trudy cautiously approached the alien canoe and looked inside of it. There, nestled awkwardly in the bow, was Bim's missing guitar.

"That's it! That's the stolen guitar!"

"How in the world . . . ? Do you think someone's been ripping off all manner of stuff from around the lake, using this old camp as a hideout?"

"If so, let's just grab the guitar and go," urged Ceci.

"Chill out," came the stern reply. "If anyone's around they would have heard us by now. We need to piece this thing together . . . and I need your brains."

Ceci considered this. Presumably, if any armed lunatic emerged from the woods to mow them down, they'd have no recourse; but if confronted by an unarmed assailant, the two of them could quickly get back in their own canoe and push off. There was no evidence of a speedboat or other motorized transport on this far shore. Trudy's rowing experience gave them an advantage; no one could outswim their return to the festival grounds.

The main concern, then, was whether there were several people (of indeterminate gender and weaponry) at the abandoned camp. The supply-laden canoe beneath the tree was a one-seater, but perhaps this spot was a rendezvous point with others.

"That couldn't be Bim's own canoe?" asked Ceci. "Did Bim perhaps stage the entire theft and sabotage as a publicity stunt, hiding her guitar over here?"

"No way," Trudy shook her head. "Bim doesn't know how to swim and would never attempt something like this. In fact, that's one of her hit songs, 'Drowning Time.' Her manager's been at her for years to take swimming lessons."

"Look at the markings, though. That canoe and our canoe are both from the festival campground. Whoever stole Bim's guitar left by water, something that never occurred to me," Ceci admitted with chagrin. "I've been trying to figure out if the thief and the saboteur are one and the same person. We could take the guitar back with us now. Bim certainly should have it, and perhaps that would flush out some confessions. Or get Rachel off the hook, at any rate. I wonder if any security guards saw this single-person canoe go out, and when?"

"Yeah!" Trudy agreed. "You know, there are supposed to be triple security workers camped by the shore on our side of the lake, and this morning we noticed that no one was around, right? Bluefern will be deeply pissed."

"Well, then," Ceci continued, "It looks like the thief waited for some distraction, or possibly staged one herself, to take the security workers away from the dock. Then she slipped off, with the guitar and some gear, heading for this place. Probably she left last night, after the storm had stopped but before dawn. Although, if you've been helping yourself to these canoes, and other women as well, the sight of someone out on the lake might look perfectly innocent even to highly alert security workers."

"And let's not forget that security crews are all voluntary, with pretty informal training. Some women sign up for lakefront security or lifeguard shifts because it sounds cushy, lying in the sun watching other women skinny-dip, you know. And then they blow off the shift when things get boring at the dock, damn it. Bluefern is really going to have a cow over this."

Ceci looked at Trudy. "There's another possibility." She squatted by the canoe and looked over its contents. "What if our getaway thief was lakefront security?"

"Huh?"

"I'm suggesting that there was no apparent security problem last night or this morning because the operator of the canoe herself had signed up to do a lakefront security shift. In fact, because it was raining so hard, she probably had no trouble getting the shift she wanted. No one else would be interested in volunteering for a wet and uncomfortable night down at the mosquitoey shore. Even if there were others on that shift, the thief perhaps told them to go get some sleep, that she'd keep watch. Then when everyone had left, she jumped into the canoe, which she'd prepared beforehand and hidden downshore."

"Well, dig that." Trudy grinned her delight. "You're just devastatingly sexy, my dear, when you play Sherlock Holmes. Now all you need is a big pipe to smoke."

"It would make me sick, but thanks, I think. Ha!" Ceci announced triumphantly. "Look here." She held up a festival security vest, which served as a cushion for Bim's guitar.

"Bingo. That's it, all right. So she was on a work shift when she made her getaway."

"Well," Ceci conceded, "perhaps not. She could have stolen the vest, too. But it makes sense."

"You know, though — oh, man, this is brilliant. If she

signed on to security at any time, Bluefern will have a record. We can get the names of all the women who did security shifts, or lakefront security, and find out who this particular woman is. Even if she used a phony name, I bet someone would be able to remember her, and describe her, too."

"This is horrible to address, but essential," Ceci said reluctantly. "We keep assuming the thief-saboteur-canoeist is female. What if it was a young man in drag? Or a young man and a young woman working together to steal from local events?"

"Food, money, technical goods, I can understand those items being ripped off by local punks. But, Ceci, why would someone steal a custom-made left-handed guitar and then smuggle it to a burned-out white power hangout? It just doesn't make sense."

And then they heard, just beyond the trees, a woman's voice, screaming.

"Oh God, help me!"

Trudy grabbed the heavy oar from the thief's canoe and crashed into the woods, shouting "Hang on, sister!"

Ceci whirled left and then right in pure indecision. Images of guns, knives, booted male enemies, and haggard storm troopers flashed before her eyes. I'm no use, she thought with anguish; I can't help. I'm afraid. I want to live. She ran back to the canoe she and Trudy had left at the shoreline.

Seconds before stepping into it, she realized: What am I doing? I can't row this thing back alone and leave my lover here to face whatever. Ceci suddenly remembered her mother's advice from stories told around the dinner table:

"And, of course, we had no weapons. We were running, running in the woods carrying nothing but our lives upon our backs. In such times, Ceci, you do things you didn't believe you could do, eat from the ground, sleep underneath a dead

body, God forbid. I was always the small one, the skinny thing, they called me, but still with quickness because I was young. So one time a man came running after me from his house, waving a rifle and shouting that he knew I had escaped and if he captured me the Nazis would pay him a good reward. Like David looking at Goliath I saw this man, his teeth as rotten as his brains, and I picked up a stone and hit his wrist where he held the rifle. And then that rifle was mine."

Ceci's mother always ended the story there, refusing to confirm whether she had, in fact, gone on to kill this man.

Ceci jumped toward a pile of stone rubble, the foundation of a burned toolshed, she supposed, and picked up two large rocks with bits of iron encrusted underside. Thus armed, she drew a deep breath and plunged into the woods.

Chapter Five

Tradition of your mothers
Waits to be shaped by your hands.
  — Faith Rogow,
  from "Mira's Lullaby,"
  in *The Courage to Dare*

Sunday morning on the other shore

Ceci ran until she felt the inevitable stitch in her side; until she felt the inevitable protest in her lungs; until a huge tree branch swiped her in the face. The woman's cries for help were nearer now, and she could hear Trudy shouting as well. She drew up sharply at a dead log and gasped. "Hey!"

Inside an ancient campfire circle pocked with crushed beer cans, Trudy was struggling with a well-muscled blond woman in faded army surplus clothes. Both of them were covered in blood. Had this woman attacked Trudy? Without even pausing to look around for armed male enemies, Ceci threw down her crude stone weapons and leaped into the fray barehanded, knocking the stranger away from Trudy and pinning her to the ground with Trudy's oversize bathrobe. "Get the fuck off my girlfriend!" Ceci heard herself shriek.

"Ceci, no. No! I'm all right. She hasn't hurt me, it's her own blood; I was trying to calm her down. I think she's cut her own wrists." Trudy, panting, pulled Ceci gently to her feet.

They both looked down at the unknown woman, who writhed and wailed. "Help me! Please, please, help me!" she moaned, and Ceci realized it was this voice she and Trudy had heard calling from the woods.

"Good God," Ceci said slowly. "I don't know what came over me, I, I saw her fighting you, and you looked like you were bleeding, and I just —"

"— went meshuggeneh," Trudy finished for her, but she was smiling. "Pretty good tackle for a nonbutch, nonjock festie-virgin, I'd say."

Ceci knelt down again and took the weeping woman's hands, which were, indeed, bleeding from the wrists. "I'm sorry, whoever you are, please, what's the matter? What help can we give you? Did somebody do this to you?"

"I just want to die," the woman sobbed.

Trudy ripped her old surfing shorts into strips and began binding the woman's cuts. "These aren't major wounds, my friend," she advised her. "As a paramedic, I've seen the real thing, and you're lucky you didn't succeed. Why did you try to kill yourself? Let me ask: Are you somehow responsible for that canoe out there with the stolen guitar?"

The woman looked first at Trudy's face and then at Ceci's and slowly answered, "You can kill me if you want to."

"Jesus!" Ceci exploded. "Listen, we just rowed over here

by accident. We're not pursuing you, we're not here to hurt you or anybody. What's your name?"

"Sandra..."

Sandra was clad in black Dr. Martens, camouflage pants, and a flak jacket. Ceci now recognized her as the lone woman who had walked up to the festival gates on the first day, carrying a huge quantity of gear on her back; Bluefern had supposed Sandra to be from the local army base.

"Are you with the army base, Sandra?" asked Ceci.

"No," the woman whispered hoarsely. "I'm from RAW."

"RAW?" Trudy and Ceci exchanged blank looks.

"You don't know about it, and for good reason," Sandra snarled. "Oh lord. Lord, lord. What am I going to do now?" She looked at her wrists, now tightly bandaged with the remains of Trudy's shorts. "Thanks," she offered. "I went crazy, because I felt so trapped, you know?"

"Tell us what we need to know," Ceci said, sitting down on the dead log and wrapping herself once more in Trudy's bathrobe.

Sandra wiped at her eyes with dirty knuckles. "I guess you're here for the festival."

"Yeah," they answered warily.

"Well, so am I. Except I was sent to the festival to blow it up. I'm a member of RAW, which stands for Revolutionary Aryan Wives. It's a white-power group."

"Oh my God," said Ceci, on the verge of losing bladder control.

"Listen," Sandra begged, "I don't believe in it anymore. I want out. I tried to kill myself because I realized I couldn't go through with it — with destroying the festival, which was my assigned mission. But now I know too much about RAW's agenda for them to let me get out of their little organization alive. I'm a recruit, see? A pledge? To prove yourself, to prove your worth, you have to do some kind of action in the name of white power, so they sent me to infiltrate this festival, as my test. They sent me because I'm not married yet. All the other women in RAW are married to men in the main group, RAM. And none of the married men would let their wives go to a lesbian festival even on a mission."

"This white-power group, they know about the festival? They've been planning to sabotage it all along?" Trudy asked.

"Oh yeah. Sure. We used this old summer camp here for meetings. Some of the men in the group used to work as camp staff, martial arts instructors, before they set the fire two years ago in the Jewish kids' bunk. The leaders of RAW were out on the lake with binoculars last summer at this time, checking out the festival and planning to maybe raid it then, but the security was too tight."

"Tell *that* to Bluefern," Ceci advised Trudy.

"So," continued Sandra, "I got involved in RAW because a friend of mine from high school married the head of RAM, and she made RAW sound pretty happening. I mean if you live around here there's nothing to do, and no work, and the white-power groups are like the only social life, which is pretty depressing when you think about it. But I got into it last year. Yeah, I got into it, read all their shit literature, convinced myself I hated Jews and black people, and lesbians. The women in RAW are obsessed with lesbians, partly because some black dykes at the army base succeeded in getting a RAW soldier discharged from their outfit."

"And your group planned to get its revenge by blowing up the festival, making you, Sandra, do all the dirty work in the name of your initiation," Ceci guessed. "I assume they counted on you not to blab if you got caught. With neither husband nor, I gather, boyfriend in RAM, you were expendable."

"What they counted on," Sandra seethed, "was that I'd be so grossed out by being in lesbian space that I'd just do the job and split. Well, that's not what happened. I cut the power all right, and I took that performer's guitar as proof, as a trophy for RAW's collection; but then as I was hiding my gear and preparing to take off I started listening to some women talking. They were having an Antiracist workshop."

"And you experienced conversion," Trudy remarked.

"Look, I don't expect you to trust me. Damn. I don't trust myself. I don't know what I think. It's more like a long twisted process of being sickened by everything the men have done to the women in my group but not having the language to express my grossed out–ness. So I'm telling you I want out of RAW, and no one gets out of RAW alive, and I have nowhere to go, and I didn't think I could exactly go to whoever runs the festival and ask for asylum after I'd wrecked the sound system."

Sandra tugged at her taped wrists. "This hurts like hell, but not as bad as this one." And she pulled up her sweat-stained shirt to reveal a fresh and gaping wound, just above her left breast.

Trudy and Ceci gasped in unison.

"It was my most recent tattoo," Sandra explained. "The one I made sure nobody ever saw, at the festival. A swastika. I cut it out last night."

"Listen, we need to get you to a doctor," Trudy interjected. "I may know how to do patch-up work but you need stitches, and there's a big risk of infection as well."

"Aren't you listening to me?" Sandra cried. "I can't go to a doctor here in town; everyone knows us because the county hospital is always treating skinheads for knife fights and survivalist bullshit wounds. Word would get back to RAW that I'd cut out their tattoo and abandoned my initiation test. I'd be dead before I left the hospital parking lot."

She swallowed. "I'm supposed to meet two guys from the group here, tonight, with the guitar and the camping gear they lent me. I figured I'd let them find me dead. That's why I cut my wrists. But first I wrote down everything I knew about the local white-power activities, and I put that in a letter with, you know, my confession, and I stuck it in the festival's suggestion box. The producers, they said they wouldn't read through the box or answer those letters until after the festival, so I figured they'd get all the information they needed to put some heat on the guys.

"And I'd be gone by then, but gone on my own terms, kind of watching over those women, you know, from the bottom of the lake."

"What about your family? Your friends? Didn't you think anyone would miss you and come looking for you?" asked Ceci.

"No, nobody, I got nobody. I wish, I wish I'd become a lesbian instead of a skinhead, you know that? I mean, I went into that festival mean as a rabid sewer rat, hating all lesbians as my enemy, but then I saw those women up close and they all looked like me. The men in my group beat the Revolutionary Aryan Wives to pulp; it doesn't matter how white you are. The men bash the women when they run out of minorities to bash. They use the Wives as practice."

Ceci sat back on her heels. More than anything, she too longed to beat Sandra to a pulp. Here, in front of her, and perhaps even at her mercy for the moment, was a woman who represented the new generation of Nazi and Klan, a woman who partook of rituals and clandestine meetings designed to plan large-scale intimidation of Jews and lesbians and people of color.

From such bored and handsome youths had Hitler's Germany been built. As the Hitler youth had informed on and arrested Ceci's parents during their student days, so the new Aryan-power hate groups in the United States were mounting, electing charismatic political candidates, painting swastikas on synagogues, denying that the Holocaust had ever occurred. Lie about history, and let history repeat unto infinity, thought Ceci.

She raised a shaking hand to slap Sandra's face, a futile gesture of spite from a lifetime of vicariously experiencing her parents' anguish. But she let her hand fall back into her lap.

For Sandra's face, at perhaps eighteen or nineteen, already wore the chips and scars from many beatings, imposed by those who privileged themselves as pure, as male.

"I know exactly what you're thinking," Trudy said to Ceci then.

Ceci stood up and walked away, toward the shore and the canoes. I don't have to do this, she thought resentfully. I don't have to be the open-minded, open-hearted Jew who embraces a Nazi as a sister, who forgives terrorism; it shouldn't be my place to make these decisions. That's not why I'm here this weekend; I'm here to find in Trudy the romantic encounter and cultural understanding I've never had before. Let someone else decide. It's not my job; I've done my work shift here.

"Listen," called Trudy, running after Ceci with a backward look toward Sandra. "We have to help this woman."

"You help her," snarled Ceci, feeling dangerously close to an asthma attack. "I'm too busy seeing my mother's face hover before me."

"And what about my mother?" demanded Trudy. "You think you're the only one here having an ethical dilemma? Okay, so Sandra cut the power and took Bim's guitar. She didn't torment anyone, didn't hurt anyone directly. We have the guitar. The power's been restored. The real question is whether we leave a young woman to be offed by Aryan pinheads, or at her own hand — or give her the dyke rehabilitation chance she obviously desires."

"Suppose she's lying? Suppose this is just a setup? Suppose we canoe her back across the lake and halfway there she knifes us both? Suppose this is just a ploy for her to get more familiar with festival structures, so she can inform on us even more meticulously and do immeasurable harm to lesbian networks?"

"Well, now," Trudy grinned. "So suddenly festival structure is 'us.' Suddenly you're feeling mighty protective toward the same festival structure you criticized last night. Suddenly you place a value on lesbian group safety as well as your own safety, or Jewish safety per se. Do you see the kind of transformation you yourself have experienced, my wee love, in a short period of time? Do you think it's possible for that same lesbian magic to awaken and politicize a young racist, a young woman without the loving intellectual family and educational privileges you enjoy?

"Because I've got news for you, Ceci: This festival and all festivals are full of women who are in recovery. They're in recovery from substance abuse; they're in recovery from domestic violence; they're in recovery from childhood rape. And to add to that, most women are in recovery from racism, meaning they've grown up in a racist society that has shaped their views and accorded them varying levels of privilege, and plenty of women oppress other women before they get wise to the antiracist alternatives.

"There are white women at the festival who haven't dealt with their shitty attitudes toward women of color; there are black women who distrust Jews and Koreans; there are Jewish dykes who haven't even begun to deal with their connection to Palestinians; and there are Asian women who trash other Asian women depending on national origin from China, India, or Japan.

"And few folks are ready to take instruction from a woman in a wheelchair; and the old woman with her cane and her repertoire of radical suffragist experience gets reduced to a quaint stereotype. No, shush for another moment and let me finish.

"Thing is, Ceci, that when you break it down thataway, no woman feels safe at a festival because there are plenty of ethnic or class or age or ability distinctions that divide us as women, and as lesbians too. But it's at a festival where you camp out with a working-class Polish dyke. It's at a festival where you hear, from the stage, performers address their different experiences in vivid and unifying terms.

"It's at a festival where the barriers bust up because we see how similar we all are, breasts, faces, voices, and that's why at a festival you can start rap groups on unlearning racism and other networking projects. Half the white women start out resenting the antiracism workshops because they think a festival's supposed to be all fun and games. By the end of a festival, if the festival's a success, maybe a few hundred women who never examined their racist attitudes before have not only changed their tune but have lived alongside the very folks they thought were different.

"Now. You're right that Sandra could be setting us up, to further some Aryan plot. But it's also true that every part of her health, mental, physical, spiritual, has been threatened by her involvement in RAW. Like an alcoholic, she's hit bottom and wants to purge that controlling substance from her life.

"So I say that while our festival has been flawed in part by Sandra's power sabotage, Sandra can give a lot back, and make the festival a political success, by telling her story and addressing the whole issue of women in hate groups. Hell, with the information she says she left in the suggestion box she can save lives. We need to get her into some kind of woman-controlled witness protection plan. Right now she needs disinfectant and gauze."

Ceci twisted a fern around her forefinger. "It's risky work to go around saving people," she said. "It's just so ironic, that this woman should be delivered into our hands, claiming that she's seen the light, et cetera, asking for our forgiveness, our absolution."

"Situation's a little too New Testament, huh?" agreed Trudy. "The sinner, born again. But I'll tell you one more thing. And, look, I don't discuss this with many other people; but I think I love you, doll." She paused while Ceci blushed in startled pleasure. Trudy's next words were not romantic. "When I was fifteen, I participated in a gay-bashing."

"You what?" Ceci's mouth fell open.

"That's right. There was a gay man who taught at my high school, and he flunked a couple of popular kids. They decided to get even and they trashed his car. I went along with them and drained out the oil. I was already good with valves and pumps then, and often called a dyke myself, but that night, I got to look normal and popular. Because I helped out the 'cool' crowd. Well, not only did we wreck the poor guy's car. When he tried to get into it the next day, he slipped on the oil puddle and had a concussion.

"As far as I'm concerned, I was directly responsible for his injury. Me, the baby dyke whose mother wanted her to become a nurse. I put a gay person in the hospital. You can bet that I fasted on Yom Kippur that year. In time, I went to that man and confessed. Did he reject me? Turn me over to the cops? Tell my mother, shame me in front of the Jewish community? No, he made me go to the gay youth group he coordinated in the next town. I've never forgotten that.

"Yeah, and he made me mow his lawn for the rest of high school, with a hand mower, not power. That's how come I qualified for my crew team; that's where my muscles, which you so admire, really come from, Ceci."

Ceci didn't say anything.

"So you see, kiddo, that I'm going to try to help Sandra. And you need to know that a lot of us are doing *teshuvah*, repenting in our own ways for early or recent ignorance. I may look like a strong and together dyke role model to you, but that's been a considerable process. If you want to know me well, let's be honest." She picked up Ceci's hands and kissed each of the fingers.

"I love you too," said Ceci.

Sandra had not moved.

"Okay, here's the deal," said Ceci. "We all canoe back over to the festival, now. We go directly to Bluefern at security, and arrange for a closed meeting of the festival producers and staff. I suppose we should invite Bim as well; she'll be delirious with joy to have her guitar back. Trudy and I will help facilitate a discussion where you can explain what you've just told us, and I think we can promise that you'll be heard.

"After that, the other festival workers may become accusatory and volatile, which is certainly their right, and Bim may want to press charges. To the best of our ability, though, Trudy and I will work to propose that no legal charges be brought against you. If you're willing to provide us with information about RAW and the white power structures you know, we'll get you into some kind of protective household.

"All of this hinges upon several factors, of course. Do you feel strong enough to face considerable lesbian wrath, at the outset, from the very community you now say you want to help? Can you withstand a probing and critical processing session with women of color and Jewish lesbians? If we help you relocate to a safer town, will you need a disguise or a new identity, and are there any legal issues that might arise, since you're under twenty-one?"

Sandra looked from Ceci to Trudy and back to Ceci again. Tears rolled down her cheeks.

"You mean you guys would help me out like that? Really?"

"As Alice Walker says, women are not guys," came from Trudy, "but yes, we want to help you out. Please note that for us it's a particular risk. We are both Jewish daughters of Holocaust survivors. I suppose your 'friends' taught you that the Holocaust never took place."

"Yeah, we had to read *The Hoax of the Twentieth Century* and that stuff. The men in our group, they sell copies of *Mein Kampf* and bumper stickers saying Hitler Was Right . . ."

"Charming," said Ceci, her eyes shut. She reached into the pocket of Trudy's bathrobe for her inhaler.

"Sandra, there's a tremendous amount of garbage you'll need to unlearn. And since you've already found the festival's workshop area on unlearning racism you know that there are women trained in such work, who can get you started. Ultimately, though, you have to make a commitment to educating your own ass righteously. Ceci and I are pretty thin-skinned about all this; we're not going to indulge you much. We will help keep you away from the people who want to hurt you."

Sandra rose unsteadily to her feet, blood seeping through her bandaged wrists and her grimy T-shirt. "Let's go, then. I want to do this. There's nothing left for me here on this side of the lake. If you can stand to, I'd surely welcome your helping me start over."

"What about some of the concerns Ceci raised?" Trudy reminded her. "If you moved away from here, took a new job in another city with perhaps a new name, would there be any questions or legal problems?"

"No one would really come looking for me," Sandra sighed. "My parents are dead. My other relatives live in California and don't even know I became a skinhead. I work for the phone company, but I can quit. I don't have a legal guardian or a trust fund or anything like that; I was living with a friend of mine from high school, but she's moving out to get married next month anyway." She looked at the ground. "If I could get my stuff from the apartment, pick up my last paycheck, and go empty my bank account, I'd be ready for anything. It would take me about two hours total."

"Fine," said Trudy. "We can work out all those details later. It's important to know how many, or how few, complications there are. Looks like we can start rolling."

They helped Sandra walk slowly back through the woods and to the beach. "Is all that stuff yours?" asked Trudy, pointing to the loaded one-person canoe.

"Some of it is equipment the group loaded me up with, survivalist tools, camping gear. I'm supposed to return it to them but —"

"Sink it," advised Ceci. "No reminders. No paramilitary anything. Just keep your personal effects and Bim's guitar."

"Okay," Sandra agreed meekly. Using a line of rope from Sandra's gear, Trudy tied the smaller canoe, still loaded, to the long canoe she and Ceci had used. "We'll all ride together in this one. Sandra, Ceci, climb on in."

"Wait!" called Ceci, who was trying to scrape the carved swastika from the old dock. "Sandra, I'm sure you have a knife or some other sharp tool you used to cut yourself. Hand it over to me, please." Sandra threw Ceci a short, sheathed hunting knife. Carefully, Ceci cut away the white-power slogans from the dock. Then, in the rough wood revealed by Sandra's blade, she carved her initials with Trudy's, entwined in a Star of David, and underneath it wrote in Hebrew: "I am my beloved and my beloved is mine."

"Amen," said Trudy.

The sun was high overhead now, and very hot. Beads of sweat gathered on Sandra's forehead as Ceci and Trudy rowed toward the center of the lake.

"Here," said Trudy.

Ceci leaned precariously over the stern of the canoe and reached into the smaller canoe tied behind. With a satisfied grunt, she pushed Sandra's survivalist kit, hunting knife, skinhead boots, sabotage wire cutters, and other offensive gear to the bottom of the lake. The heavy pieces sank instantly. "There," said Trudy. "Not you, but your former life, resting far below, harming no one." She resumed rowing.

"I'm sorry," Sandra sobbed, her head buried between her knees. "I'm sorry, I'm sorry, I'm sorry."

"Hang on," Ceci urged, feeling torn. "We'll be back at the festival soon." She patted Sandra's shoulder for a brief moment, then picked up her oar. For the rest of the journey, no one spoke.

The green hills of the festival camp beckoned them now, and they could hear laughter ahead, squealing children, ritual drumming. I am coming into the Promised Land, and bringing a little lost pharaoh with me, thought Ceci. Was it only this morning that Trudy and I made love here, in this very canoe? And only last night that I made love with a woman for the first time? I am jealous, possessive, and lustful; I want Trudy all to myself today, I don't want our remaining hours spent in the complex company of others. I want to lie in a hammock somewhere and feed her grapes. Mmm. I know the work that must be done here. I understand why Sandra should be helped.

But me, I'm awakening to so much simultaneously. It's not like physics research, where certain basic experiments have certain basic outcomes one may rely upon. At this festival all my assumptions have been challenged. I need time. And I want Trudy's hands on me again.

The canoe ran aground in the reeds, and Trudy hopped out, lending an oar for Sandra to grasp. Ceci sensed that it would be wise not to attract too much attention and, forsaking modesty, removed Trudy's bathrobe and wrapped it snugly around Bim's guitar. Naked, she pulled the canoes ashore and then followed the other two women up toward the path.

By now new security workers were posted at the dock, and they whistled and hooted good-naturedly.

"Hey, there! You're not supposed to use the canoes," one woman yelled.

"You! Babe! How come you didn't sign out when you left your shift last night?"

"Sorry," Sandra called back, hiding her bandaged wrists behind her. "One of the canoes broke loose, so we took the other canoe out to rescue it." She hurried her pace.

"Good save," Trudy muttered.

"I've done nothing but tell lies for two years," said Sandra. "It's all I'm good at."

They tried to keep their faces expressionless as they walked toward the producers' cabin behind the main stage. At Trudy's cabin, Ceci stopped for a moment to retrieve her clothes and her overnight bag, now quite dry. "But you're welcome to stay with me again tonight," whispered Trudy, "so that I can give you all the undivided attention you deserve."

Bluefern sat on a folding camp chair, making notes on her

clipboard. Her lively face looked tired and worn from anxiety and guesswork, although the many crushed paper coffee cups around her feet suggested that caffeine had kept her working longer than humanly possible.

She jumped up to slap a mosquito, and gave a startled squawk, for there in front of her stood a most unlikely trio: three grave-eyed women covered with dirt, blood, and leaves. Bluefern recognized the youngest woman from opening day at the gate. "What's up?" she asked casually, twirling her pencil.

"I think we've found your saboteur," Trudy smiled. "Bluefern, meet Sandra."

"I don't believe it," Roz shook her head. "A nineteen-year-old white-power activist?"

"Believe it," shrugged Bluefern, rubbing sunburned shoulders against the cool metal siding of the sound equipment trailer. Trudy had taken Sandra over to the Womb for first aid, and Ceci was on her way to Bim Daring's cabin with the precious guitar. "She says she wants asylum, and I've called for a four o'clock meeting with all the workers, backstage."

"Blue, you can't be serious," exclaimed Nicky. "This person nearly succeeded in killing our star performer! We need to get her off the land and into the hands of the authorities!"

"And what authorities might those be?" inquired Bluefern. "The local Klan-affiliated cops? Men in uniforms with nice handcuffs? Men in uniforms with nice tranquilizers? Jesus, we spend the whole festival talking about alternatives to patriarchal structures, and when push comes to shove, we're ready to play into their hands. Look, I'm as freaked out as you about this, but let's hear the kid out. She's in pretty sad shape; apparently she felt so trapped she tried to kill herself last night."

Nicky and Roz exchanged looks. Both of them worked part time as volunteers on a gay hotline in their home city. They often received frantic calls from suicidal teenagers. "I think I need a large, large sandwich, a pail of sun tea, a list of all festival workers, and that confession letter this Sandra person stuffed into our suggestion box," said Roz. "Nicky, who's that woman in Chem-Free who used to work for the Cleveland crime patrol?"

"Janet?"

"Yeah! Let's get her over here. And get Gina, too. Get that therapist from the Crones Tent who works with delinquent girls. Get our festival lawyers, they're probably at the goddess circle, and, let's see. Can we keep this quiet until all the workers are here for the four o'clock meeting?"

"Sure. In fact, the two women who brought Sandra in suggested that. They're escorting her to healthcare and will be back later."

"A really good, large, large sandwich," repeated Roz. "All right, then. Put Josie in the golf cart and send her around to announce a workers' meeting at four."

Ceci, back in her own clothes and carrying Bim's guitar, took a shortcut through the crafts area and suddenly caught sight of her reflection in a full-length mirror. She was amazed by how much she had changed in the past two days. Fierce brown eyes peered out of a brown face. Her breasts stood out against her white shirt, and the marks of Trudy love bites covered Ceci's neck and throat.

And I have Trudy under my fingernails as well, thought Ceci with embarrassed relish. Look at me. Today I am a lesbian. It's like becoming bat mitzvah all over again; I should buy myself a present. Ah. Later. She hurried along to Bim's cabin.

At the gate, Ceci encountered the same security guard who

had brought Rachel to her the previous night. "Hi, it's me," Ceci sang out. "I'm not looking for Rachel. This time I need to see Bim Daring."

"Sure you do, hon," chortled the guard. "Everyone wants Bim. You'll have to do better than that!"

"I've recovered Bim's guitar," said Ceci, peeling away the bathrobe covering to reveal gleaming frets. "Can I take it in to her?"

The woman's eyes widened. "Wow! You stud! Where the heck did you find it?"

"It's a long story. I know Bim's been quite anxious. Would you walk me to her cabin?"

"Oh go ahead," waved the security worker. "You'll make her day; she's right over there. Boy, is that a load off everyone's mind! Congratulations!"

Ceci tiptoed up onto the porch of the first performer cabin. "Ah, hello," she called. "Bim? My name is Ceci. I have something for you."

"Who's there?" called a muffled voice.

"You're going to be wonderfully surprised!" Ceci couldn't keep the lilt from her throat. The cabin door was slightly ajar, and Ceci boldly took a step inside . . . only to behold what no festiegoer, producer, performer, or security worker had seen for six years. The sight of Bim Daring in bed with Carrie Marathon.

Chapter Six

I will call off my guards if you will
I'll uncover my heart
I will give you my hand, I will
Together we'll start
Together we'll start
— Jamie Anderson,
from "Borders"
in *Center of Balance*

Where compassion dwells, love is blossoming.
— Mimi Baczewska,
from "Open Door"
in *Turning Tide*

Melissa spent a sleepless night regretting her words to Ceci. In no way had she meant to bait Ceci's sensitivity about being an outsider. The question of sabotage seemed, at the time, more important than the social etiquette of polite conversation. Was Ceci really involved in military intelligence service, as her Ph.D. exam notes, still neatly stacked in the tent corner, suggested to the paranoid eye? On the other hand, what sort of spy would be that obvious, leaving her own protocol files about? It didn't make sense.

Perhaps Ceci was merely completing a required course in code theory, relevant to her atomic studies. Still . . . what sort of lesbian chose the field of atomic studies? That brought Melissa right back to the plaintive judgmental inquiry she'd made the night before: *What sort of lesbian are you?*

And now Ceci had disappeared. If indeed she was a hired infiltrator, involved in the sabotaging of women's culture, the entire festival might be at risk. On the other hand, if Ceci was as innocent as she claimed, and as new to festival phenomena, then Melissa had blundered hugely, alienating a bewildered festie-virgin who needed support. Either way, Melissa felt responsible, accountable, panicky. When night became morning and there was still no sign of Ceci, Melissa's insomnia turned into guilty sobs.

What she did not expect was to see her lost tent-mate come striding confidently through the woods nude, covered in hickeys, with a stunning six-foot woman in tow.

Ceci found Melissa weeping into her sleeping bag exactly as Melissa had found Ceci on their first day of the festival.

"Ceci!" Melissa managed to say. "You're okay! I was worried, you know? I wasn't sure if you had your little inhaler with you or *what*. And I never, never meant to speak to you so. Please forgive me for my impulsive accusations last night. Let's clear up all these misunderstandings right now."

"Gladly." Ceci crawled into the tent and rearranged her plaid sleeping bag, pulling Trudy inside with a purr of lust and a long, deep kiss. Melissa observed this astonishing performance in open-mouthed wonder.

"Pleasure to meet ya," Trudy nodded, her callused hand never leaving Ceci's ass.

"Melissa, this is Trudy, another nice Jewish girl and another daughter of survivors." Ceci smiled momentarily into Trudy's eyes, then continued. "I'm sorry if my abrupt departure last night caused you concern. Wow. Oy. Was it only last night? So much has happened in a brief space of time. I feel as though I've acquired psychic jet lag, moving so rapidly from one life-changing experience to another . . ."

"Yeah, it's always like that at a festival," Trudy added cheerfully. "One's personal itinerary ends up looking like this: Meaningful moment at noon, political conversion at two-fifteen, random food anecdote, performer encounter at five, weather mishap, overnight fling at ten. The next day's agenda might include a festival controversy, minor injury or insect attack, guilt trip about breaking some rule on the land, reunion with long-lost honey, expensive crafts purchase, drumming frenzy, and perhaps a processing power surge under a tree with workers later on. Do you dig me?"

Melissa watched as Ceci and Trudy roared with laughter, slapped one another on the back, exchanged veiled looks of arousal, and generally made themselves at home. This certainly didn't seem like the behavior of an antilesbian spy or prudish newcomer. What had happened to Ceci in the middle of the night?

"Melissa," Ceci finally explained, freeing her tongue from Trudy's, "we've solved the mystery. Or, rather, the young woman responsible for attempted sabotage came into our care through an unexpected series of events, and in another hour we're meeting with all the workers to discuss whether she should receive sanctuary.

"Though your little interrogation last evening hurt me deeply, I must thank you for forcing me out of the tent and into the parentheses of festival politics. In my wanderings since last night I've encountered women with their own complex relationships to festival community and festival policy, and I've found that my petty festie-virgin discomforts are mild in comparison.

"I want to thank you for bringing me to this festival, Melissa, otherwise I'd never have met that host of instructive characters, including Trudy. I think I've learned that the only antidote to feeling like an outsider is relentless participation. As the rabbi said, 'It is not up to you to complete the task, but neither are you free to desist from it.'"

"Then . . . some other woman really did try to wreck the festival? There was an attempted infiltration?" Melissa asked, watching Ceci's face closely.

"Yes, the sacrificial lamb of a local hate group, unfortunately," Trudy confirmed. "We're hoping to get her into a witness protection program, lesbian-style."

Ceci knew what still weighed unpleasantly on Melissa's mind. "Melissa," she said in as straightforward a tone as possible, "you were correct in presuming that the U.S. Intelligence community has an interest in me. This past spring I completed an optional academic course in code theory, and my language abilities alerted a team of military intelligence recruiters who occasionally scout for talent at MIT. These nefarious gentlemen approached me in a roundabout way with offers of work. I turned them down; I've no interest in their little covert operations.

"You see, I know only too well that during the nineteen fifties the United States intelligence community recruited and sheltered Nazi war criminals; perhaps persons who tortured my own parents long ago. After World War II such individuals became 'valuable' to the American science establishment. Cold War politics, and the post-Hiroshima arms race in silos and nuclear technology, changed American science; made Communism, rather than Fascism, the monolithic opponent patriotic scientists had to outsmart.

"If a few ex-Nazis could help to defeat the Soviet Union, could provide information about Soviet physics, did the State Department care? And so the most brilliant of the Nazi torturers, those scientists and engineers who concocted the cleverest of experiments, were spared judgment and given new identities in the science world. Here.

"Part of my chosen work in science has been a personal mission — I study the influence of those exonerated Nazi scientists on American nuclear physics and scientific language. I also monitor the location of such craven scientists for the Wiesenthal Center and other anti-Nazi organizations, although nearly all the hidden scientists are deceased now. Because I grew up speaking German, it's been easier for me to pursue my controversial research discreetly.

"Someday soon I'll be publishing the ultimate expose of U.S.–Nazi atomic collaboration. But to crack the codes used by the original postwar teams, I had to learn some mathematical war-games language. So, Melissa, those are the suspicious-looking study notes you riffled through while I was sitting in a Porta-Jane."

"Oh," said Melissa in a small voice. "How come you didn't tell me all this last night?"

"Because I'm tired of vomiting up my life as the daughter of survivors to satisfy others' political criteria. Because I don't discuss my work with everybody. It's just as complex, personal, and dangerous as other forms of professional activism. Because I've encountered countless brainy-girl stereotypes in my life, each less flattering than the one before, and I simply won't play any more.

"Better you should decide for yourself that I'm one of the good guys, or good gals. I'm not going to make that correct conclusion easier for you by reconstructing my ethnic past, or my past as a gifted schoolgirl in the sexist world of science.

I'm sick of other lesbians' sympathetic voyeurism toward my difference."

"Amen," from Trudy.

Ceci rose. "And now, Melissa, I think we're all a little wiser. There's plenty more to tell you, but let's go over to the food tables and get lunch, yes? This afternoon's meeting will be long and no doubt draining as hell. I could use a big bowl of tofu right now."

"Well!" Melissa spluttered, accepting the hand Ceci held out to her. "I never thought I'd hear you crave tofu, either." She lowered her voice to a whisper. "Personally, I've been dreaming about a plate of ribs smothered in hot sauce."

"I heard that," yelled the animal rights activist in the next tent.

At four o'clock a weary, perplexed stream of workers began to seep out of the woods and toward the backstage security campfire circle. Although neither Ceci nor Trudy wore the striped wristbands identifying festival crew workers, they were permitted into the compound as Bluefern's special witnesses. This was Ceci's first immersion into the backstage workers' community. She felt a momentary covetous outrage toward the free-flowing cocoa and — could it be? — free onion bagels available to work crews round the clock.

Under the summer boughs of a tree sat Sandra, motionless on a hard folding chair. Curious workers took their places on hay bales, stumps, and logs, nodding hello to the festival producers and crew coordinators. In the close quarters of so many bare backs, Ceci once again marveled at breast structure and the plethora of sweet-smelling body oils. One woman had painted her mastectomy scar to look like a horse and rider galloping across her torso. Another's countless piercings made rainbow-patterned lights dance on a shiny metal trash can nearby.

Near the workers' freestanding showers, hundreds of multicolored towels hung limply on wooden pegs.

When Rachel entered the circle, Ceci could not resist jumping up to whisper in her ear.

"You're off the hook! We've found the woman responsible for cutting the wires; Bim's guitar is safe too. Nobody's going to investigate you any further. I can promise you that."

"You didn't tell them about . . . the baby?"

"Nope. And if that makes me a festival sinner too . . . well . . . so it's between me and the Goddess on the Day of Judgment." They sat down as Bluefern called the tribunal to order.

Without introduction or fanfare, Sandra rose and began to tell her story. She described a lonely adolescence of abuse and battering in a series of foster homes, rebellious flirtations with a group of handsome young athletes, her shock at finding out their political views, and her own gradual acceptance of that white supremacist dogma as the young men praised her pure Aryan qualities. There were audible gasps and cries of outrage from the assembled workers as Sandra outlined the real agenda of RAW and RAM and the groups' role in burning out the Jewish summer camp years before.

"Go on," said Trudy, clenching Ceci's hand.

Sandra then explained the ultimatum she'd received from her so-called friends: a dangerous initiation rite that required her to infiltrate and blow up the lesbian festival. If she failed, chickened out, or told, she would be killed. If she accomplished the mission and, like Dorothy retrieving the witch's broomstick, brought back the lead performer's guitar as proof, she would pass the initiation test and be married to one of the male group leaders, thence to begin bearing Aryan children.

Ceci tried to imagine Sandra's choices: Kill or be killed, marry a violent hatemonger or disappear under his colleagues' fists. Sandra deserved no award for her awkward attempt at sabotage; certainly many festiegoers might have died that night. But Sandra had found seeds of resistance somewhere within herself; had actually made the unexpected and never-articulated choice: to identify with the "enemy" she was sent to oppress.

When Sandra faltered for a moment, Ceci and Trudy took over, explaining how they had happened to find Sandra, her near-suicide attempt, their own mixed feelings as daughters of survivors. Bluefern confirmed that Sandra had voluntarily turned herself in to security, and Roz and Nicky, the festival producers, added that they were reluctant to press charges, to bring local police into the festival's business.

Her eyes tightly shut, her dirty fingernails digging into her kneecaps, Sandra concluded her recitation with a request for sanctuary, and held up the crumpled confession she'd jammed into the festival suggestion box. "Here's the start of my repayment schedule," she said. "All the information about where and when their meetings are, damage done over the years, dates of incidents, pseudonyms, weapons storage sites, stuff like that. I can testify against those guys . . . maybe. But I need a safe place to get my act together first. Can you help me?"

Immediately there was an uproar.

"Excuse me, folks." Trisha, who taught African drumming, now took the floor. "I've had about all I can take of nurturing wounded white women. I mean, you all can quit poking me with a fork, 'cause I'm done. Here's a fool who nearly killed us all, and we're negotiating as to how to make her feel better? You'll pardon my saying so, but we already spend too much time trying to forgive and soothe white women after they've victimized people.

"I know there's a good movement on this land of white women challenging their own racism. But I feel that in so many situations — like this kangaroo court, here — I'm asked to understand, forgive, say 'Oh honey, must be really tough to carry those prejudices around.' What about us women of color, raped and killed and colonized by this girl's buddies over time? Great for her to see the error of their ways; but don't

117

ask me to be her welcome mat. I don't feel safe with her here."
She sat down to many calls and finger snaps of approval and
support.

"Alice, you run the Antiracist workshop tent here. Do you
want to respond to that?" asked Roz.

"Yeah, if I may." Alice was big, wide, red-haired, her feet
resting now on her lover's buttocks. "I hear Trisha's point.
What I want to add is that if we believe our own rhetoric, that
all white women are racist to the degree that they've grown
up in this race-biased culture, then we'll have to purge not
only Sandra, but also Roz, Bluefern, me, and on and on. Just
about everyone at this festival whose face is white has been
guilty of practicing racism through acts of commission, acts of
omission, words, deeds, thoughts.

"At one point or another the women's movement brought
us all together and that's why we're in this space today; not
to give Sandra absolution for her past, but to keep her alive
for her future. There're men outside this festival waiting to
jump Sandra. Do we score any antiracist points, morally, by
sacrificing Sandra to them? And if we consign Sandra to the
local police instead, well, sad to say, the county police here are
supposedly hand in glove with the county Klansmen, unlikely
to press the charges Sandra might raise about the Aryan
movement.

"Now wait." She leaned forward, rolling a cat's-eye marble
in her fingers as she spoke. "Here at festival we have support
services for women in recovery from alcoholism; for women in
recovery from drug abuse. We acknowledge in twelve-step
programs that those past behaviors hurt and harmed other
people. No telling who in the Sober tent drove drunk once and
killed a child. That's a private burden. We would never throw
a dyke out of this festival because she once fucked up with a
hit-and-run. Our problem is that Sandra's fuck-up is so fresh,
so recent, so close to our hearts.

"Her recovery from racism, so to speak, will be a lifelong
rehabilitation there's no twelve-step program for right yet.

And Sandra's coming forward gives us a rare chance to judge, to play cop, a power trip we might easily inflate, laying all symbolic flaws at her feet. But I see a scared youngster who was talked into criminal mischief by some deeply abusive boys. I want safe sanctuary, Trisha, for all women here —"

"Time," Nicky interrupted, holding up her watch.

"But we always end up excusing a white woman's acting out because she was abused or molested, and pack her off to therapy so she can feel better, while my community heals alone," began Trisha.

"Yeah, God damn it, I was molested," Sandra spoke up. "I, I know I'm supposed to be done talking here, but . . . it's true, my parents beat the shit out of me, and then my foster dad and my boy cousins had their way too. That's why I moved out when I was fifteen. In a way those white power dudes were the first family support I had. I mean, I was valuable to them because I was blond and stuff."

"And you needed love and approval so bad you agreed to blow up the lesbian nation, huh?" sneered one of the carpenters. "Really touching. I spent all summer building that stage. You're dangerous, kid. I say get her out of here."

And so it went. Ceci watched with mingled fascination and bewilderment as each worker rose in turn to make an impassioned speech for or against Sandra's sanctuary. "We call this processing," Trudy whispered in resignation as three different Jewish lesbians, each claiming that they represented the Jewish lesbian viewpoint, argued Sandra's case.

"You know the saying: three Jews, four opinions," Ceci whispered back.

One faction of white workers came forward and confided that they, too, had once belonged to a "white student union" before joining antiracist work. "Gee, that makes me feel so much better about all this," sighed Gina, the coordinator of the Women of Color tent.

"She's being sarcastic . . . right?" Ceci heard one of the workers whisper.

The festival lawyers talked about liability and litigation.

The sound and light crews listed, in excruciating detail, the damage Sandra had done to festival equipment and the potential for electrocution of all workers present during the sabotage.

Bluefern wanted to know why Sandra was able to cut wires during her work-shift; why was there no crew supervision, so close to the stage?

Nicky and Roz called upon Janet, the off-duty policewoman from Cleveland, to assess Sandra's eligibility for a witness protection program.

The Women of Color and the Jewish women workers argued about who felt more threatened by Sandra's presence.

The stage carpenters vowed to walk out if Sandra remained.

And workers from the Antiracist tent wanted Sandra to go on the night stage to tell her story for all festiegoers to learn from.

The shouting, weeping, cross-accusations and impassioned rhetoric made Ceci's ears ring.

In the middle of the confusion, Bim Daring and Carrie Marathon arrived.

"Well, look who's out of bed," chortled a security worker.

"I don't believe it," murmured another.

"Are they, like, together again?" said a third.

Bim held her guitar up high, like a baton. "Women!" she yelled. "Goddess babes. Friends of many years. Be it known that B. Daring and C. Marathon herewith propose to play a reunion concert tonight in celebration of — of — well, our reunion. All old favorite songs and suchlike requests will be honored. We also propose to donate our combined festival earnings as night-stage artists; the festival may retain said fees for repair costs to sound and lighting."

She glanced blandly at Sandra. "Girl, you came close to

destroying me the other night. But I've spent many years destroying myself, in far more demoralizing ways. If you hadn't ripped off my guitar I might not have blundered into Carrie's life again. Well, I've got my guitar back. And I've got Carrie back as well. I'm not in the mood to press charges."

Bluefern's face was a warm moon rising, all the tension and responsibility of security work rewarded by this unanticipated watershed in women's music. "Oh, Bim. Hot damn. We'll get you whatever you need. Tea, keyboard backup, the best monitors. Night-stage crew, go set up for their sound check. Wait: And one of you better get their lyrics to L. B. or Sherry so they can interpret this set. And Laverne to get the introductions ready. And —"

"Bluefern, we're in the middle of a meeting here," complained one of the electricians. "We can't drop everything and party with Bim and Carrie."

"If I can't dance, I don't want to be part of your revolution," Bluefern quoted. "Emma Goldman, right?"

In the end there was no consensus but much compromise. The workers all agreed to remain at the festival an extra two days for a special intensive session on security measures and future work-shift policy. Janet agreed to take Sandra back to Cleveland, where Sandra would remain in her custody until a lesbian safe house and new identity were arranged. Sandra agreed to a year of community service with Janet's hate-crimes unit, using her skills from the telephone company to monitor organized hate groups. Three women from the Cleveland area who ran an Antiracist study group agreed to work with Sandra on a regular basis. And the festival producers agreed to write a formal report on the incident, protective of Sandra's identity, which would be sent to every festiegoer three months after the festival, inviting feedback, suggestions, and strategies for other issues of festival infiltration.

Ceci stood up and found her clothes were soaked with sweat.

Trudy also looked wrung out, pale. It was over. For now.

They walked away from the meeting and toward the lake again.

To distract the festiegoers during the long tribunal, Josie and a few other workers had organized an afternoon carnival with games and athletic competitions. Ceci could see women covered in mud, playing nude volleyball, several circles of Hackey Sack, a fierce rugby match, wheelchair tennis, and basketball.

Beyond the main lawn, on the slippery softball diamond, an intensive batting clinic attracted many women. Apparently the clinic instructor had finished the teaching portion of her workshop and was now offering free kisses to anyone who could hit her fast ball.

"How tasteless," Ceci frowned as an eager festiegoer passed the word along. "Some professional jock takes advantage of the festival to humiliate dozens of women, striking out all but those noteworthy few who pass the test and win a sexual experience? That's not a skill clinic. It's entrapment. She'll probably throw an easy pitch at whomever she finds attractive."

Trudy rolled her eyes. "Come on, Ceci, no one's being forced to go to bat. I know, you have old and painful associations with softball. But for many athletic lesbians, sport *is* sexuality. There's physical pacing and effort and exhilaration common to both. If a hotshot pitcher wants to sweeten the festival with some exhibition moves and warm kisses for those who can best her, well, who wouldn't be turned on? Look.

Everyone's heading over there; she must be something else. Let's go see."

They followed the traffic of amused, aroused voyeurs to the backfield diamond, where a handmade sign announced: HIT MY PITCH AND WIN A KISS. WALK-INS WELCOME. Ceci uttered a mild snort of contempt and perched on a bleacher, hoping that Trudy would soon prefer bed to bat. They were just in time to see the present batter finish her turn with a futile eruption of dirt clods as the gleeful catcher roared, "Strike! No kiss!"

And there, on the pitcher's mound, stood Mary Leigh Davis.

The sight of her, Mary Leigh the mythical dream girl from Ceci's adolescence, was so hugely unexpected that at first Ceci could not focus on her old fantasy/nemesis with any practical comprehension. Rather it was as though Mary Leigh's physical outline, enhanced by the strong sun shining behind her, was burned onto Ceci's retina, etched in raised silhouette. A familiar pattern slid over Ceci's new festival persona like the transparency sheets used in overhead projector instruction.

Ceci felt, rather than saw, Mary Leigh's image on her eyeballs; felt, too, the instinctive throb behind her nose where Mary Leigh's last pitch to Ceci had homed. What did it mean, that Mary Leigh appeared here, now? Had Mary Leigh been at the festival all this week, pursuing her own festival agenda, so that her path and Ceci's might not have met at all? What forces had led Mary Leigh to attend this festival? Could it be that she, too, had taken a lesbian path? Within that context, might she and Ceci now meet as equals, or would the same harsh pattern from yesteryear be superimposed, with Ceci as the awkward and brainy baby dyke and Mary Leigh as the softball ace with butch privilege and confidence?

123

These waves of thought crashed through Ceci's mind in less than two minutes, a wholly unanticipated tsunami of emotions and decision-making. It can't be. It can't be. I mustn't give myself away, say anything. Oh, my face, it's burning already, oy. No. Stop. I don't want to find Mary Leigh again, not here! Not now! It's Trudy I want, Trudy, Trudy, her warm breath under my chin, her Jewish wisdom, her eyes of sparks.

I'm being inducted into the tribe of lesbians; I can't afford to go into the person I once was. Old crushes, old humiliations, pain, baiting, taunting, ah, she broke my nose. Look at her. Look at that pitch. *Boom!* There goes another festiegoer, laughing, defeated, retiring with ease because she has no emotional connection to Mary Leigh. She isn't playing for kisses, present or past, just loving the game. Taking the dare.

Well, I can't watch this. I can't watch. Ceci's heart was racing, her fists clenched. How many years had it been since that fateful meeting between both their sets of parents? Eight? Nine? Mary Leigh was here, now, beautiful, mischievous, tall; waiting, on the mound, for the next player. It would be so easy to run away, to keep adolescence an angry memory, and not to see the grownup who had replaced that former Mary Leigh.

"Are you all right?" Trudy was asking anxiously. "Whoa, girlchik, what is wrong?"

Without answering, Ceci walked up to the plate. Her footing was steady as she crossed the muddied softball diamond, but she felt cold sweat and hot sweat simultaneously seeping from her limbs, trickling down the insides of her arms, and coating her palms. When she reached the plate she knelt to rub the crumbly earth into her hands, then wiped her palms again onto her hard knees. She kept her head down for another moment, not yet ready to have Mary Leigh see her, recognize her, call out to her in whatever etiquette of ghastly or tender greeting this strange reunion required. Below Ceci's glance, home plate yawned up, a simple reminder of every haunting dream, resonating echoes of that last afternoon in the park nine years before.

Trudy, not quite comprehending the drama before her, silently picked up the lighter of the two bats from the grass and handed it to her lover.

Batter up.

"Piece of cake," sang Mary Leigh, who had nimbly pitched slow and hard ball all day to any number of festiegoers.

"Serve it up then," croaked Ceci. Mary Leigh scowled, flexed her massive arms, wound up, and delivered a deceptive curve ball.

Ceci grunted, swung — to no avail.

"Shit, girl, don't gear up for a Caribbean breeze until you've met my tornado," Mary Leigh laughed, and scooped up another ball with large hands. "Get your foot off the plate, for one thing. Here it comes, stamped and addressed. You gonna give it back to the post office?"

"Come on, Mary, lay it in here, nice and easy," the catcher behind Ceci yelled. "Whiff her, you don't need kissing."

"Stay in the batter's box," Trudy hissed from the sideline.

Ceci tried to lower her center of gravity, to keep her feet from sinking into the lumpy mire chopped up by former batters. The second pitch seemed to fly to her head like an angry hornet. She found herself ducking instinctively: not my nose! Not my teeth! Not my head, I need those brains. Damn.

"Strike two," sang the catcher, who wore an old university softball jersey with DORIAN on the back. "Come on." And in a whispered, sympathetic aside to Ceci: "Make her pitch to you."

At least one hundred women were now bobbing up and down in the bleachers, like so many surfers riding the engrossing tension of Ceci's bid for success. Encouraging shouts rang through the air: "Cork one!" "Pound on it!" "All you, baby!"

Dorian flipped the ball back to Mary Leigh and whistled. Mary Leigh wound up for the last pitch. Think! Ceci castigated herself, frantic. What do I have to match Mary Leigh's confidence? What was my part of our after-school bargain? I was the tutor, the scholar, the nerd. Yeah, the science nerd, all the years since then still locked up in books. Physics books. Motion theory.

Aha.

Suddenly Ceci saw the walls of her beloved lab at MIT in her mind's eye, the complex theories hand-written as poster charts, formulas memorized almost unconsciously through daily exposure. An object in motion tends to stay in motion. At object at rest tends to remain at rest. Weight, time, gravity, inertia; space, target, arc, position, mark. Physics graph charts; what had the past academic years been but an exercise in scientific calculation? Such were the skills Ceci owned now; skills readily applied to the path of a ball through the air.

Make her pitch to you.

Velocity. Speed. Arc. What's the density of the air? How many pounds of pressure is the pitcher applying? Distance in meters between us?

Shivering with excitement, Ceci sneezed, just at the moment Mary Leigh's arm came up and over. The sound of that sneeze was familiar to Mary Leigh: familiar, enough, to jerk her elbow laterally with surprise, sending the pitch precisely low enough for Ceci's calculated force to make contact.

And then, the unmistakable sound of wood smashing leather into the next county, and the one hundred festiegoers screaming their awe for the scrawny science dyke who stood with the bat ringing power from her fist.

"Hey!" gasped Mary Leigh, who had at last come to recognize Ceci's face. "Hey, aren't you . . . ?" She pulled off her glove and shook her head, staring, uncertain, still.

"So kiss me, God damn you," Ceci said.

* * * * *

For an hour, they walked around the land together. Whatever was said or not said between them no one ever knew, for not even Trudy was invited along. And whether there were more kisses between them, Trudy never asked.

Sometimes the past offers up a live ghost to those who have been haunted. For Ceci, meeting Mary Leigh at the softball plate was the beginning of a better kind of story, a personal script with, at last, some personal swagger to it. No longer would Ceci see all strong women as rivals, as bullies; for she had elected herself to their office of strength on her own terms.

At the end of that long walk, Mary Leigh, now a gym teacher and coach of the best lesbian softball team in Pennsylvania, went jogging through the woods until she found the ball Ceci had hit. "I think," she explained to Trudy, "that this should go into the Lesbian Herstory Archives. But I might just bronze it and keep it on my desk for a while."

Much later, Ceci, Trudy, Mary Leigh, Melissa, and kitchen worker Jen sat on damp logs in the rear of the concert field as Bim and Carrie played a reunion concert to enthusiastic cheers. The sun stayed warm and high until nearly nine P.M., and all the canceled and interrupted stage sets from the festival weekend finally resumed, concert after concert. Bim and Carrie were the last to go on, their unannounced reconciliation startling long-time festiegoers into a frenzy of nostalgia.

"More! More!" shrieked a gray-haired fan to Ceci and Trudy's left. "I came out to their albums," she explained, "after I'd raised three kids and a couple of horses, in Texas. Went to their Austin concert wearing a disguise. I was that nervous: I used the wig from my daughter's Halloween outfit! Hearing Bim and Carrie live like this again, it just reminds me of all my own great, first awkwardness." She turned shining eyes on Ceci, almost without seeing her, then lifted her chin toward the stage once more. "Does anyone forget their first encounter with women's music?"

"I'm right in the middle of mine," smiled Ceci, marveling that she had arrived at this festival afraid of being unpopular. Both Trudy and Mary Leigh were now vying to feed her chunks of carrot cake, while Melissa stroked her back. "This is my moment of complete conversion." She stretched out her red-sneakered toes and gave a yowl of luxury.

"It isn't all games and backrubs. But I suppose I needn't tell you that," Jen added. "This festival has been about as real as it gets." She looked at Melissa. "About time, too!"

"The pleasant memories are just as real as the processing drama. From festival to festival I manage to forget the stress incidents and remember the epiphanies, don't you?" Trudy asked Melissa.

"For sure. Like the smell of the ferns. The crushed ferns that result from setting up a tent in these woods." Melissa blushed. "Yeah, I'm a city kid, but out here I find myself thinking soupy poetic lines I'd never dare say in my neighborhood at home. Every year when I arrive at this festival I go about the business of making camp like a poker-faced dyke, all business and tent stakes, while secretly my mind is gushing 'These dear woods!' and stuff like that . . ."

They all giggled.

"As for my own first impressions," Ceci contributed through a mouthful of cake, "they were animal rather than vegetable. What I will recognize and think to myself next year when I arrive on the land is 'These dear breasts!' " She gestured fondly toward the rows of shirtless women in lawn chairs.

"You're not a festie-virgin any more," said Melissa. "Already planning on next year, and referring to the festival as *the land*. Do you even hear that festival vocabulary, now, coming from your lips?"

"I've got another surprise for you. Next year, I'll be returning as a worker. I think I should put my science skills to good use, and branch out into new festival skills simultaneously." Ceci looked around at all her friends. "So I've agreed to train as a sound engineer with the women's production companies in Boston this winter, and next summer I'll be coding and programming a new sabotage-proof sound system for the festival!"

"Then you're coming back to Boston with me after all. But, Ceci — won't MIT seem impossibly male dominated to you after this festival? I mean," Melissa risked saying, "you've gone through so many changes. Look at you. Surrounded by lesbians, and finally at home with that. It's hard for me to picture you back among the techno-boys, bowing to their sexist attitudes. Do you still want that? Is a Ph.D. worth all their bullshit?"

"Oh, Melissa, please," sighed Ceci. "I don't want to sound like Mr. Spock, but you're not being logical. Do you hear what you're saying? You wish the scientific establishment wasn't so male dominated, so, rather than encouraging the one woman scientist you know, you discourage her from completing her doctorate. As though keeping women out of the hard sciences protects lesbian interests.

"I don't want the sciences to be controlled by powerful men who experiment on women and children's bodies, who postpone breast cancer research, who play with plutonium. But my remaining ignorant, my remoteness from science, wouldn't guarantee my safety. Better to see what the boys are up to, to challenge them, blow the whistle on them; and soon. I might even invent something new and beautiful myself.

"Let me ask you this. You work in a women's bookstore. Presumably, all the books sold there are somehow relevant to feminist interests. Yet when we first met at your place of work, I was searching for texts on women and science, and few of the bookstore staff could assist me. You'd read little from that genre; were far more conversant in poetry than physics. What do you do when a little schoolgirl comes in to browse? Do you consistently steer her to the arts rather than the sciences? Perhaps because you, too, believe that science would be too 'hard' for a young reader, or that science isn't an appropriate field for a budding feminist?"

"Well, uh," from Melissa.

"Ceci, don't shame the woman in public," Trudy warned, invoking an excellent point of Jewish law. "Give her a break."

"Sorry." Ceci smiled gently at Melissa. "I'm just busting your chops, just whaling on you, because you're an easy mark. Right?"

"Touché."

"Anyway, you two can continue this dialogue all year long, in Boston," Trudy reminded them. "And I'll serve as a referee, when I'm up from Baltimore visiting Ceci. Let's stop processing and listen to Bim and Carrie now. This is my favorite song."

Ceci leaned back into Trudy's arms, feeling their protective bulk. She looked at the shining eyes of the women in the audience, many of whom were singing along with Bim and Carrie, old lyrics apparently well known to most. This is my bat mitzvah, she thought again, and smiled. Today I am a lesbian.

The Moral of the Story

This is a work of fiction, and the characters and their conversations are imaginary, with the exception of certain obvious references to actual lesbian artists and institutions. It was musician/belly-dancer Jamie Anderson who first suggested that I should try to write "festival fiction," and I acknowledge her influence with much appreciation. My intention has been to mirror the real concerns and political issues I have heard discussed around campfires and during processing sessions at differing festivals.

I began attending women's music festivals in 1981, shortly after my twentieth birthday, and went on to become a worker, then a coordinator, then ultimately a performer myself. When I wrote the first draft of this story in 1992, over twenty women's music festivals and retreats were held annually in the United States between March and October, ranging in size from intimate gatherings of two hundred or less to the five-thousand-plus city of women that makes the Michigan festival unique. Brand-new festivals were still emerging in the early 1990s, and older festivals had not quite begun to disappear.

When I first began writing *The Question of Sabotage*, I was years away from producing my larger nonfiction book on festival culture, *Eden Built by Eves*, and I had barely made the transition from festiegoer to festival worker myself. I had complete confidence only a few years ago that festival culture would last forever and that a trip to a festival was an essential pilgrimage for all American lesbians.

The first-timer is often overwhelmed by festival culture — perhaps bug-bitten, uncomfortable, soaking wet, politically challenged, afraid of saying the wrong thing, crushed out on somebody, self-conscious in new shirtlessness. This is Ceci's dilemma in the story, and while Ceci is hardly intended to symbolize all festie-virgins, her struggle to achieve the ease of a seasoned camper does reflect my empathy for the alienated newcomer. No amount of friendly outreach can appease the dislocation some campers feel upon entering a matriarchal superstructure for the first time. Socialized by homophobic and misogynistic institutions to hide our woman-affirming identities, lesbians usually blossom in the freeing environment of a festival, but adjustment to that freedom of expression takes time.

Festivals strive for diversity and for providing safe space in the interests of all women. The question of multicultural representation is often painful; many festivals are overwhelmingly white. In this story I have centered key issues around Ceci's Jewish identity, for that is the ethnic location from which I myself speak. Ceci's confrontation with Sandra symbolizes the complex future that lies ahead for festival workers: In a racially stratified society plagued by hate crimes against women, lesbians, and all people of color, are we prepared to deal effectively with violence at a festival? Are we prepared to welcome women who are unlearning racism? Whose job is it to educate, to forgive, to trust? Should festivals give sanctuary to those women who recently exhibited oppressive behavior? Who decides?

In fact, these are the conversations I have heard around festival campfires every year since my first journey to Michigan. And so I reiterate that while Ceci's story is fiction, the setting is real; the possibility for sabotage is real; and we are our own best answers to the questions raised.

What I could not foresee was the slow disappearance of many beloved festivals. I once routinely attended Sisterfire, Northeast Women's Musical Retreat, East Coast Lesbian Festival, Northampton Lesbian Festival, Rhythmfest, Virginia Women's Music Festival, Heart of the West Festival — all of the above now gone or at least suspended. Robin Tyler's Southern and West Coast Music Festivals are no longer held, nor is Tam Martin's Pacific Northwest Jamboree. Amazingly, some much smaller regional festivals, notably the Gulf Coast Festival at Camp Sister Spirit in Mississippi, have survived. But these transitions have placed enormous pressure on the two longest-running festivals, National {since 1974) and Michigan (since 1976) to be all things to all participants. Michigan in particular has been under assault by transgender activists for its womyn-born-womyn policy (a policy I support), even as it also staves off attacks by right-wing or just plain hostile straight critics. The National festival is at present facing considerable financial debt.

And so, the fable I created is quite relevant. Ultimately, there is much work to do to ensure that our community is not destroyed from within — by quarrels, factionalism, racism. I'm committed to seeing that festival culture lasts another twenty-five years. I extend that challenge to the interested reader, who is invited to show her support by getting involved. Now. An online source for womyn's festivals is <http://www.xpn.org/amazon/festival.html>. Following are the contact addresses for three long-running festivals that need our ongoing support.

See you next year!

Easter Weekend:
    The Gulf Coast Womyn's Festival
    Camp Sister Spirit
    Box 12
    Ovett, MS 39464
    <sisterspir@aol.com>

June:
    The National Women's Music Festival
    P.O. Box 1427
    Indianapolis, IN 46206
    <wia@indynet.com>

August:
    The Michigan Womyn's Music Festival
    P.O. Box 22
    Walhalla, MI 49458
    616-757-4766
    OR:
    P.O. Box 7430
    Berkeley, CA 94707
    510-652-5441

See you next year!

Bonnie J. Morris

About the Author

Bonnie J. Morris teaches women's studies at George Washington University and Georgetown University. She is the author of the Lambda Literary Award Nominated *Eden Built By Eves: The Culture of Women's Music Festivals* as well as two books on Jewish women's history, and she is a contributor to more than fifty books and journals. Morris is well-known on the women's music festival circuit as a worker, lecturer, stage performer, fan and archivist.

Publications from
BELLA BOOKS, INC.
The best in contemporary lesbian fiction

P.O. Box 201007   Ferndale, MI 48220
Phone: 800-729-4992
Web:www.bellabooks.com

ROOM FOR LOVE by Frankie J. Jones. 192 pp. Jo and Beth must overcome the past in order to have a future together.
ISBN 0-9677753-9-6 $11.95

THE QUESTION OF SABOTAGE by Bonnie J. Morris. 144 pp. A charming, sexy tale of romance, intrigue, and coming of age.
ISBN 0-9677753-8-8 $11.95

SLEIGHT OF HAND by Karin Kallmaker writing as Laura Adams. 256 pp. A journey of passion, heartbreak and triumph that reunites two women for a final chance at their destiny. ISBN 0-9677753-7-X $11.95

MOVING TARGETS: A Helen Black Mystery by Pat Welch. 240 pp. Helen must decide if getting to the bottom of a mystery is worth hitting bottom.   ISBN 0-9677753-6-1 $11.95

CALM BEFORE THE STORM by Peggy J. Herring. 208 pp. Colonel Robicheaux retires from the military and comes out of the closet.
ISBN 0-9677753-1-0 $11.95

OFF SEASON by Jackie Calhoun. 208 pp. Pam threatens Jenny and Rita's fledgling relationship.   ISBN 0-9677753-0-2 $11.95

WHEN EVIL CHANGES FACE: A Motor City Thriller by Therese Szymanski. 240 pp. Brett Higgins is back in another heart-pounding thriller.   ISBN 0-9677753-3-7 $11.95

BOLD COAST LOVE by Diana Tremain Braund. 208 pp. Jackie Claymont fights for her reputation and the right to love the woman she chooses.   ISBN 0-9677753-2-9 $11.95

THE WILD ONE by Lyn Denison. 176 pp. Rachel never expected that Quinn's wild yearnings would change her life forever.
ISBN 0-9677753-4-5 $11.95

SWEET FIRE by Saxon Bennett. 224 pp. Welcome to Heroy — the town with the most lesbians per capita than any other place on the planet!   ISBN 0-9677753-5-3 $11.95

Visit
Bella Books
at

www.bellabooks.com